"If this is a joke, it's not very funny."

Alex Ramage's voice was harsh. "You knew perfectly well that I expected a man."

Beverley stared back defiantly. "Does it matter whether I'm a man or a woman as long as I'm able to do the job?"

He gave a bark of laughter. "Have you ever dealt with an angry stag or fed a couple of wildcats?"

Beverley gazed at him speechless. There was something in his voice that made her blood run cold. And there'd been nothing in the advertisement about wildcats!

"Ah, I thought not!" His mouth curved in a humorless smile. "Then I suggest, Miss Nesbitt, that you return home— immediately."

What a fool she'd made of herself. If only she had known what she'd be up against. But one thing remained certain: she would stay on Kinneil...despite Alex Ramage!

HENRIETTA REID

is also the author of these

Harlequin Romances

Many of these titles are available at your local bookseller.

For a free catalogue listing all available Harlequin Romances
and Harlequin Presents, send your name and address to:

HARLEQUIN READER SERVICE,
1440 South Priest Drive, Tempe, AZ 85281
Canadian address: Stratford, Ontario N5A 6W2

Lord of the Isles

by

HENRIETTA REID

Harlequin Books

TORONTO • LONDON • LOS ANGELES • AMSTERDAM
SYDNEY • HAMBURG • PARIS • STOCKHOLM • ATHENS • TOKYO

Original hardcover edition published in 1981
by Mills & Boon Limited

ISBN 0-373-02442-8

Harlequin edition published November 1981

Printed in U.S.A

CHAPTER ONE

HER suitcases at her feet, Beverley sat on the rough stone wall of the pier and idly watched the hectic activity as people and cargo disembarked from the car ferry.

She had been one of the first down the gangway of the *Maid of the Islands* and hadn't really been too worried when she had seen that there was no one there to meet her. She had heard how casual the people of the Hebrides were about time; never particularly worrying if they were not too punctual. And no doubt the two Miss MacCrimmons, at whose guesthouse she was to stay, would be equally casual.

She watched with interest as her fellow passengers were greeted by friends and relatives, effortlessly switching from Gaelic to English as the occasion demanded, their voices soft and with a musical lilt.

When everyone had disembarked, a group of Highland cattle were driven aboard. They were wild-looking animals with wide pointed horns, and long ragged hairy coats of a rich rust colour. They looked fierce and untamed, and for a moment she was put in mind of the buffaloes she had seen in films of the American West, but she had been told that these animals, in spite of their looks, were as gentle as lambs.

When the cattle were aboard, and the excitement had died down, she began to look around a little anxiously. The *Maid of the Islands* showed every sign of departing for the next island on its route and there was no one there but herself, seated on the wall with her two suitcases, while the gulls swooped and screamed mournfully above the aquamarine waters of the little port.

She slipped to her feet and looked around.

There was no doubt about it, she thought, Kinneil was an enchanting island. Grey stone houses piled upwards on the slope behind her, while beyond that were the mountains, patched with gorse. Could Alex Ramage, by any chance, have forgotten to arrange for her to stay with the Miss MacCrimmons at Kinneil Guesthouse? He had written that Miss Morag MacCrimmon herself would meet her at the pier. Perhaps he was elderly and a little absentminded, she thought with dismay. Nevertheless, he had accepted her and that was all that mattered!

Beverley had always wanted to see the Hebrides and the idea of a working holiday had appealed to her. She had seen his advertisement for an assistant on a project in connection with the ecology of Solan Island, a small island off the coast of Kinneil. She had answered, hardly daring to hope that she would be accepted, because she had no practical experience to offer. But he had accepted her. And now here she was, and here she intended to stay, until someone came to meet her, or until she found some alternative mode of transport.

A cloud came between her and the sun, and Beverley pulled her coat closer about her throat. In the shadowed light there was now something rather dour and forbidding about the little port with its rough stone walls, and its few workmen going about their duties about the ferry, occasionally darting curious and, to her mind, suspicious glances in her direction. They didn't need the suitcases at her feet to tell them that she was a stranger because on an island like Kinneil everyone was known, and a strange face was a subject of speculation.

She began to walk up and down, as chill air drifted across the water. She would simply have to find her own way to the guesthouse, she decided, and was on the point of questioning one of the men about transport, when there came the sound of an ancient car bucketing along the dusty road. It shuddered along the quay and came to an abrupt stop. The door was flung open and a thin bony woman appeared. She wore an ancient tweed hat under which appeared a mass of fuzzy white hair. She had a weathered and forbidding appearance and as she advanced towards Beverley she studied her with a sharp assessing glance which took in the cases at her feet.

With a frown, she came to a halt. 'And who are you for, if I may ask?' she asked abruptly. 'I'm supposed to meet a Mr Beverley Nesbitt. At least, that's what Alex Ramage told me.' She sounded aggrieved.

Beverley held out her hand with a smile. 'I'm Beverley Nesbitt,' she told her. 'And I'm to work with Mr Ramage on Solan Island. You'll be Miss MacCrimmon, I'm sure. Mr Ramage wrote to me that you would meet me.'

Miss MacCrimmon regarded her incredulously. 'But it was a *man* I was to meet,' she informed her bluntly. 'Beverley is not a girl's name.'

'Well, I'm afraid it's mine!' Beverley told her, smiling placatingly at the scrawny, irate old lady. 'Beverley's a family name, although I admit it doesn't sound particularly feminine.'

'Ah, that's it!' breathed Miss MacCrimmon. 'But how Alex Ramage will take this when he finds out I don't know! Well, I suppose nothing can be done about it now. You'd better come along and explain it to him yourself. It's none of my business!'

Brooding heavily, she turned and indicated the car with a wave of her hand, and began to stalk back towards it.

Beverley picked up her luggage and meekly followed. When she had placed her luggage in the boot, the car was started and juddered forward with a grinding of gears.

'It seems to me that you must not have made it clear that you were a female.' Miss MacCrimmon stared straight ahead as she steered the car into a narrow winding lane. 'Alex Ramage gave me one of the letters to post and it was addressed to Mr B. Nesbitt. Alex is a hard man, and won't take kindly to being deceived, I can tell you that.'

Beverley was silent. Yes, it had been a mad thing to do. And she had no excuse—at least not one that would cut much ice with this harsh old lady!

There would be no point in telling Miss MacCrimmon that she had Hebridean blood in her veins from her mother's side of the family and that, even as a child, she had listened enthralled to stories of the misty Isle of Skye, where wild violets and golden kingcups grew in such profusion; a land of magic where water horses come out of the lochs to create terror in the hearts of children; where the little fairy women who live in the hills come at night to assist with the housework, so that the kitchen is swept and clean when the housewife awakes in the morning. Skye, abounding in stories of Bonnie Prince Charlie, gay and fearless, the 'yellow-haired laddie' of song and story!

Miss MacCrimmon sniffed. 'It seems to me you won't be long here. Alex Ramage will soon send you packing. But you've only yourself to blame, you know.'

But Beverley was getting a little tired of being put on the defensive. 'I don't see why he shouldn't accept a woman if I can do the job. After all,' she said sarcastically, 'there's no great strength needed to check on bird boxes, or list wildflowers. Actually I'm quite good at that sort of thing.'

Miss MacCrimmon gave a short abrupt laugh. 'No doubt, but you're not familiar with wildcats, I presume.'

Beverley sat up with a start. 'Wildcats?' she asked blankly.

'Aye. No doubt you'll come across them. They're part of the fauna of Solan!' Miss MacCrimmon told her heavily, casting a sly sideways glance at her companion to spot her reaction.

She must have been quite satisfied, Beverley thought, aware that her jaw had dropped at the news.

'He seems to be a man with a great many interests,' Beverley said dryly. Already she was beginning to dislike

Mr Alex Ramage intensely, yet she had the strange feeling that Miss MacCrimmon rather admired and looked up to him, to judge by the tone of respect in her voice when she mentioned his name.

'Ah yes, Alex Ramage has a great many interests. But then he's a very clever man. He's a scholar, you understand, and has written books about his travels in different parts of the world. But he has very strong views when it comes to women. He's not one of those modern types, you know, who think women are fit for everything. To his mind it's a man's work. And you could tell him till you're blue in the face that you'll be able for the job, and he won't believe you. And quite right too!' she snapped.

Beverley sank back. Her little spurt of defiance had evaporated. She felt depressed and apprehensive in spite of the beauty of the scene. They were driving along the coast road. On one side lay machair while on the other lay a strip of pearly white sand bordering a sea of dazzling aquamarine water.

'Here's the house.' Miss MacCrimmon pointed to a tall white-painted house that had the gaunt unadorned look of Morag MacCrimmon herself. It was only as they drew nearer that Beverley saw that the garden was filled with masses of strange exotic-looking shrubs and blossom-covered pergolas. 'What a beautiful garden!' she exclaimed.

Morag nodded and for the first time a smile touched her thin lips. 'Yes, everyone who comes says that. Not that I take much interest in it myself. My sister Isa is the one with green fingers.'

But as the car stopped with a jerk Beverley was in no mood to enjoy Isa's efforts, for apprehension overcame her at the thought of meeting her new boss.

As they walked up the crazy-paved path bordered with masses of fragrant velvety wallflowers Beverley saw a short, very stout little woman standing on the doorstep. She looked a little puzzled as she watched them approach, Morag stepping out ahead and Beverley following with her cases.

Morag gave a short harsh laugh. 'I expect you're wondering who I have with me, Isa. This, if you please, is Beverley Nesbitt. It turns out she didn't inform Alex that she is a female.'

In spite of her embarrassment, Beverley could hardly restrain a smile as she saw the sisters together, Morag so tall and gaunt and weatherbeaten while Isa was short and plump with soft pink cheeks.

'This is my sister Isabelle,' Morag announced, turning to Beverley. 'She's the one who will show you to your room and see to anything you want, until,' she added grimly, 'you get things sorted out with Alex Ramage, and we know exactly where we stand.'

Beverley nodded, feeling her spirits sink to zero. What Morag was telling her was that her stay at the guesthouse would be of short duration, as soon as Alex Ramage discovered the deception.

She was relieved, however, to discover that Isa was not taking things as seriously as her sister. Her manner was easy-going. 'Come away in,' she said comfortably. 'You look perished. And as to Alex Ramage—well, he'll just have to get used to a girl assistant. It'll do him no harm. In my opinion, he needs some of the rough corners rubbed off!'

'Alex is a very clever man, and it's not for us to criticise,' Morag interposed rather sternly.

'I'm not saying he isn't a scholar!' Isa said hastily. 'But you must admit, Morag, he's not very well mannered.'

'He doesn't mince his words. He's sincere, not two-faced! Besides, he has his mind on other things than manners,' Morag told her.

'Well now, I'd better show you to your room,' Isa cut short her sister's remarks by taking one of the cases from

Beverley. She led her up a steep stairway laid with a flower-patterned carpet to a narrow upper hall with a polished floor. She flung open a bedroom door and Beverley looked around in pleasure.

The room was like something from a past age. On the floor was well-polished linoleum. To one side, under the sloping ceiling, was a brass bed with a crisp white frilled valance at the head. Beside it was a hand-made rug patterned with apple-blossom.

Isa put down Beverley's case beside the huge Victorian wardrobe and, crossing to the bed, folded down the snowy linen sheets, and felt the mattress with her short plump fingers. 'Duck-down!' she announced. 'Morag and I dry the feathers in the sun, and I must say there's not a modern mattress can match it for comfort.'

'It's a lovely room!' Beverley exclaimed, glancing about in appreciation, and noting with pleasure that beside her bed was a pretty ruby-glass oil-lamp.

'I'm afraid we've no electricity here,' Isa said regretfully.

'Oh, but I prefer the lamp,' Beverley assured her. 'Somehow it suits the room.'

Isa beamed at her. 'It's not everyone who likes oil-lamps, you know. Oh, and another thing, before I go. I must tell you that the water here comes from a well and is not always very reliable. Sometimes the pump goes out of order. But if you want a bath, just let me know and we'll fix you up somehow or other.'

Beverley crossed to the window, hung with brightly patterned drapes that matched the cushions and chair covering. There was a magnificent view of the sea and of an island which seemed to be covered with a mist of yellow flowers and a froth of palest green foliage.

Isa joined her. 'That's Solan,' she told her, 'where Alex Ramage is doing his studies.'

'But what are those yellow flowers?'

'Primroses,' Isa told her. 'Parts of Solan are so thick with them that you can't walk without stepping on them.'

'Does anyone live on Solan Island?' Beverley asked.

Isa shook her head. 'Not now. But there is still a "black house" there, and Alex Ramage sometimes stays there overnight if he's particularly busy instead of coming back here.'

'He stays here, then?' Beverley enquired.

'Oh yes. We do our best for him, but Alex is not an easy man to——'

But at this point Morag's harsh voice could be heard calling up the stairs.

'I'll have to go,' Isa broke off. 'I'm sure you'd like something to eat. Come down as soon as you're ready. There's a fire in the parlour. In an old house like this you need it, even at this time of the year. The bathroom's at the end of the corridor. The water's nice and hot at present, if you want to freshen up.'

The bathroom proved to be as old-fashioned as the rest of the house. There were bright brass taps and a high-pedestalled hand-basin. The bath was a huge affair, encased in mahogany. The water however was hot, although it was faintly brown, as though peat-stained.

When she had washed and put on a fresh blouse, Beverley felt better able to face the coming interview with Alex Ramage. Would he be joining her for the meal? she wondered nervously.

But when she went downstairs and into the small parlour with its maroon wallpaper and glowing peat fire, there was no sign of him. A small round table with a white linen tablecloth that hung to the floor had been pulled near to the fire and as soon as she was seated Morag marched in with an enormous tray bearing all sorts of interesting and savoury dishes. This must be what she had heard described as 'high tea'—a great favourite with the Scots, her mother had told her.

First of all there was a big brown teapot, its glaze crackled with age, then dishes of finnan haddie, fried haggis and tomatoes, and a rich wedge of cake that seemed mostly composed of currants enclosed in a thin layer of pastry. This must be black bun, she guessed. Apart from that, there were honey and jams and an assortment of cakes and scones. Was she really expected to eat all this? Beverley wondered in amazement.

As she placed the dishes on the table, Morag said briskly, 'Just you tuck in now, and don't go in for any of that slimming nonsense! It's all good wholesome food. We make the jam ourselves with fruit from the garden. None of that rubbishy shop-bought stuff!'

'All the same,' Beverley smiled, 'even if I had an enormous appetite, I'd hardly be able to get through all this.'

She found, all the same, that she took more than usual, for the food was delicious. And as she ate she gazed around with pleasure. This was just the sort of parlour that the Kinneil Guesthouse should have, she decided. The paintwork was brown and worn, but there were bright flowering plants on the windowsills: on the wide comfortable armchairs were embroidered antimacassars. A faded brown photograph of an old gentleman in naval uniform gazed down a little sternly above the mantelpiece. It seemed to her to be a typical Scottish guesthouse, homely, with many years of use, yet spotlessly clean and without any pretensions.

The finnan haddie was delicious, smoked, and tangy with mustard sauce, and she finished off her second cup of hot strong tea with a muffin generously smothered in the MacCrimmons' blackcurrant jam.

She drew one of the broad comfortable armchairs up to the fire and leaned back. The turf glowed crimson without a flame. And, now that the tide was out and the surf no longer broke on the shingle, there was a deep comfortable silence.

This calm was broken, however, by the sound of a door crashing open. Heavy footsteps strode across the hall and a deep resounding voice called.

A moment later came Isa's voice. 'Yes, Alex, what can I do for you?'

'Well? Did someone meet Mr Nesbitt?' he asked impatiently.

There was a short pause, and Beverley guessed that Isa was finding difficulty in answering the question. 'Morag did go down to the ferry,' she replied reluctantly, 'but it turns out to be a she.'

'What on earth are you talking about?' The resonant voice sounded irritable.

'Simply that it's *Miss* Beverley Nesbitt.'

'But that's impossible!'

'Well, that's the way it is, I'm afraid, Alex.'

'Then I assume she was sent about her business and returned on the ferry?'

Isa sniffed. 'No then, indeed she was not! She's in the parlour, having her tea, if you want to know. And now, if you don't mind, Alex, I've things to do in the kitchen.' And Beverley heard Isa hurry away.

There was a short pause, then heavy footsteps slowly advanced, and Beverley found herself being regarded by an immensely tall figure. His head seemed close to the low ceiling of the little parlour, and his broad shoulders almost filled the width of the doorway.

For a moment surprise took away her dread of the coming interview. How like a Viking he looked! As if he had stepped out of one of the pictures in her school history book. One of the fierce Norsemen who in olden days had come in their long boats to plunder the West coast of Scotland.

He stared at her in disbelief for a moment or two, then strode forward, and she found herself gazing into a face that was not strictly handsome, yet had a strength and force that would instantly command respect. The deep-set eyes under thick black brows were anything but friendly. 'What's this?' he asked harshly. 'Some sort of joke?'

Beverley swallowed. The meeting was turning out even worse than she had feared. Somehow, when she had accepted the job she had not thought her deception so serious. After all, she knew she was capable of being a good assistant.

'Well, why don't you speak up? You knew perfectly well, from my letters, that I expected a man. Why didn't you tell me?'

Immediately Beverley became defensive. She stared back at him defiantly. 'What does it matter whether I'm a man or a woman?' she demanded, 'as long as I'm able to do the work satisfactorily!'

He gave a bark of laughter. 'It seems to me you haven't the slightest idea what you were letting yourself in for. Do you think I'll allow my assistant to spend her time sitting by a cosy turf fire when a storm blows up? And do you really feel fit to deal with an angry stag or feed a couple of wildcats; cats that can't be tamed, and with sharp claws that can rake you like a razor?'

Beverley gazed at him speechless. Somehow when Morag had mentioned the wildcats they hadn't sounded so very terrible, but there was something in Alex Ramage's blunt statement that made her blood run cold.

'Ah, I thought not!' His mouth curved in a smile that showed no humour. 'Well, now that's settled, I suggest you go home immediately!'

He swung around and in a few strides reached the door. 'Isa!' His voice boomed through the hall. 'Miss Nesbitt is leaving right away. Ask Morag to drive her to the ferry.'

Through the open doorway Beverley could see Isa, her cheeks flushed. 'The ferry will have gone by this time,' she told him tartly. 'Anyway, even if it hadn't, Morag wouldn't take kindly to making the journey again. And I can't say I blame her.'

Alex Ramage frowned. 'Well then, she can leave by tomorrow's boat.'

'I'll go when I want to,' Beverley called defiantly, although she noticed with annoyance that her voice had a distinct tremor. There was something so elemental about this man. It was as though he imposed his will upon all he met.

As he re-entered the room she jerked up her chin. 'I intend to see something of the Hebrides, now that I'm here. Solan Island looks so pretty, I'd like to explore it.'

He glared at her. 'So you'd like to explore it! You think Solan's such a pretty place! So romantic to wander around in—as though you were on a perpetual picnic! But it's not all primroses. Parts of it are bogs almost twenty feet deep, and on the north are sheer cliffs that fall into the boiling surf. Explore it by all means, but remember this—if you're foolish enough to meet with disaster I have no intention of rescuing you.'

Anger swept through Beverley. 'You needn't worry,' she broke in, 'I shan't ask you for any help. And as for acting as your assistant, why, I wouldn't take the job now, not if you paid me a thousand pounds a week!'

And with this, she stalked from the room with as much dignity as she could achieve.

As she mounted the stairs she could hear his voice in the hall. 'I'm going to the village to see if the outboard motor is fixed. I'll probably stay on and lend a hand, if Hamish hasn't got it ready, so I shan't be back till late.' Then came the thud of his footsteps crossing the hall and the slam as the door closed behind him.

In her own room, Beverley stood at the window, gazing out with eyes that were clouded with tears of disappointment.

So her trip to the Hebrides was at an end, almost before it had begun! And what was she going to say to her family when she returned? They had warned her that she would probably land in hot water by her deception. But she had been so sure she could persuade her future employer that she was fit for the job.

But then she hadn't known what sort of man she was up against! If only Alex Ramage had been an ordinary reasonable sort of person, she could have talked him into giving her a trial. She realised now that she had been visualising him as a studious sort of man, a scholar, thoughtful, kindly and open to persuasion. It had all been wishful thinking. What a fool she had made of herself, she thought wretchedly. She could only hope that their paths would not cross again before she left on the following day. Not that it was likely. She would make her little excursion to Solan Island and be back before he returned from the village.

She looked around the pretty, spotless room regretfully. She would have been happy here, she felt sure. It was easy to like Isa, and she had the feeling that Morag's bark was worse than her bite.

Just then there was a gentle tap on the door and Isa came in, her pretty plump face crumpled with distress. 'I can't tell you how sorry I am that you're going,' she said. 'It would have been lovely to have you staying with us, but in a way perhaps, for your own good, it's just as well. You couldn't have endured Alex Ramage as your boss; you can see for yourself he's quite impossible. We've had all sorts of people staying with us over the years, some of them quite difficult, mind you, but never anyone like Alex. He thinks of nothing but his work and has no patience with anything that interferes with it in the smallest way.'

'Well, I suppose I've only myself to blame!' Beverley said ruefully, as she crossed to the window and gazed across at the enchanted Isle that would have been her place of work if things had turned out as she had hoped. 'I should have let him know the truth, and then I shouldn't have made this useless journey. But I did so long to get the job; it's just the sort of thing I should have loved. Do you think I could see the Island before I go?'

'There's no reason why you shouldn't,' Isa said bracingly. 'The tide's out now and it's only a mile across the sands. All the same,' she warned, 'you'll have to be careful. The tide comes in suddenly and, with the boat out of order, you would be quite cut off.'

'I shan't stay too long,' Beverley promised. 'I don't want to cause any more trouble than I've already done.'

CHAPTER TWO

WHEN Isa had gone, Beverley changed into comfortable walking shoes and a tweed skirt and set off.

She enjoyed the walk immensely. Herring gulls swept against an azure-blue sky. In the sands under her feet were shells of the most delicate colours; pink, lilac and palest yellow. She stooped to gather some of the prettiest.

As she drew near to Solan Island she could see ahead a barrier of sharp rocks, covered with lichen and slippery with seaweed. But she discovered that by walking along the strand she was able to curve around the end of the island and to come into a beautiful little crescent of smooth white sand. Behind it were dunes and a moment later she found herself on that carpet of primroses she had glimpsed from her bedroom window. The flowers grew so closely together that it was impossible not to crush some of them as she walked.

Soon she found herself in a little copse of birch trees and here the ground was carpeted with the blue of wild hyacinth. The air was scented with the snowy blossoms of white hawthorn. Overhead skylarks trilled and from the distance cuckoos called.

How glad she was that she had made the effort to explore the Island. It would have been sad to have returned home without seeing this beauty.

To the east of the island she found a hillside patched with bracken and sprinkled with silver birches and rowan trees where a stream dashed down over rocks streaked with white quartz, and for an instant she glimpsed the rough red coat of a deer as it dashed into a little valley leading upwards in the hill.

The island was larger than she had expected and here and there she saw the remains of stone walls, showing that at one time it had been inhabited. But the only house standing was a strange primitive building formed of stones laid one upon another with no mortar binding them. The roof was curved and thatched with straw in which there was one black patch where smoke had escaped through a hole. There were no eaves to this house; instead the thatch seemed to be tucked down tightly into the thick inner wall.

This must be the black house Isa had mentioned. Curiosity overcame her, and cautiously she went in.

And now she saw how it had come by its name, for the walls were blackened by many years of turf smoke. There was only one tiny window covered with dust and cobwebs, but it was enough to let her see that Alex Ramage didn't believe in making himself comfortable. The dull reddish ashes of the fire lay undisturbed. In a doorless cupboard she saw stacks of tins and piles of unwashed crockery, while in one corner lay a mound of empty cans.

In great contrast was the way he cared for the specimens of his study.

Against one of the walls was an erection of wooden shelves, and here all was neatness and order. In glass jars were what looked to her like pieces of seaweed, each neatly labelled with the name, first in Latin and after that in

English. The names 'bladderwrack', and 'bootlace weed'
caught her eye. She moved along peering into the various
jars and drew back a little as she saw one in which spiders
moved against the weed. On this was written *halorates
reprobus*—but whether this was the name of the spiders or
of the seaweed, she could not tell.

On another shelf were shellfish. And now Beverley no
longer tried to decipher the Latin names, but read,
'common cockle, razor shell, striped Venus, netted dog
whelk'. A tiny white shell was labelled only by its Latin
name, *'neolepta sulcatum'*, and she wondered what the
natives of these Hebridean islands called it. Surely they
must have some lovely and romantic name for this delicate
little shell.

There were specimens of worms too, one of which she
noticed was called 'peacock worm'. There were various
plants and grasses and even some beetles, one of which
looked like a tiny very pretty ladybird.

How typical of the man, she thought as she gazed
around, to be so careful of his scientific specimens, and so
indifferent to discomfort.

She picked her way across the room and explored the
cupboard. It had obviously been rescued from an attic—
one of the MacCrimmons' discards, probably! A battered
plastic basin had been placed on the top shelf, and beside it
a rather grubby glass-cloth. Beverley pulled open one of
the drawers. Here she found a mug, tins containing tea and
sugar and the remains of a loaf, stale and brick-hard. Yes,
Alex Ramage's life on the Island was extremely primitive!

Feeling a little ashamed at the thought that she was
prowling, she stood uncertainly in the middle of the floor.
She wanted to see something more of the Island, yet she
was reluctant to go. Somehow she couldn't bear to leave all
this disorder behind her and she felt an overwhelming
temptation to tidy things up. After all—She bit her lip
thoughtfully. After all, even if Alex Ramage resented her

interference, he could do nothing about it. She would be on her way home before he discovered what she had done.

At the thought she couldn't restrain a giggle. What was the name in the Hebrides for the little fairy women who come out of the hills at night to tidy up the kitchen for the tired housewife? Then she remembered—brownies! Did Alex Ramage believe in brownies? she wondered. Somehow it didn't seem likely. Anyway, it would give her satisfaction to put things to rights and, taking off her jacket, she placed it on a large packing box that served as a table, and looked around.

First of all she gathered the ashes on sheets of an old newspaper, and carried them outside. Where to put them? There was no dustbin, of course, so she was forced to place them in a thicket of bracken.

Next she would wash the dishes, she decided. She took the basin down and going to a stream that flowed near to the house filled it to the brim with the clear sparkling water. She found that a handful of coarse bracken made a useful scrubber and in a short while had the crockery gleaming and stacked it back in the cupboard. She also disposed of the empty tins. Then, gathering some twigs from a little copse of trees, she piled them up in the fireplace and placed over them small knobs of peat which she found piled against the outside wall.

When she had finished she surveyed her handiwork with approval. She wasn't really concerned, she told herself, whether Alex Ramage would find his quarters more comfortable. She had done it to satisfy her own home-making urge; for her own pleasure—nothing else!

She glanced at her watch and gasped as she saw how time had passed. Remembering Isa's warning, she dashed out and hurried as fast as she could, stumbling sometimes on the rough ground, until she came once again to the rocky shore.

She stopped, gazing on the scene with horror, for now

everything looked different. Where the rocks had been dry, they were now covered with water.

If she had stopped to consider she would have realised that it was much too late to attempt a crossing, but fear and excitement drove her forward. Her foot slipped as she scrambled across a boulder now slimed by sea-water and she crashed down against jagged rock on to a ledge beneath. For a moment she lay there stunned, then pain in her leg returned her to reality with a jolt and she discovered that it was gashed below the knee. Panic gripped her. She would have to remain until the tide went out. And when would that be?

She felt reassured at the thought that the Miss Mac-Crimmons knew where she was and would send help. But immediately she felt icy fear grip her as she remembered that the outboard motor was out of order and that Alex Ramage had gone into the village to assist the unknown Hamish to fix it.

She tried to get to her feet, but found it impossible to walk; the pain was too great. She sat back against the boulder, feeling the chill of the early summer evening.

It was easy now to visualise Solan Island in winter, when surf rose high in the air and crashed on the shore. And as the sun dipped lower there was something mysterious and uncanny about the island in the twilight, and she remembered about the wildcats and glanced around fearfully.

It was then she thought she heard the faint put-put of an outboard motor. She strained her ears. Was she just imagining it? But soon she dimly discerned a boat advancing: in it, Alex's unmistakably burly figure. Surely there could not be two men on the island as tall as he!

As relief set in, she had another worry. How was she to face him? Probably when word had got around that she was missing he had managed to get the boat hurriedly fixed. The kind of situation, she felt certain, which would put him in a bad temper!

It was impossible for him to land at the point where she

was seated and she watched as he steered the boat past, heading for the little strand. As he disappeared from view, she waited with growing tension. Then she could hear the sound of steps clambering over the rocks. Soon his figure, seeming gigantic against the afterglow, loomed out of the height behind her.

'So you managed to get stranded! This is exactly the sort of thing I expected!' were his first words.

There was a certain satisfaction in his tone which irritated her, and she found that she would have preferred anger. He wasn't even taking her predicament seriously, she thought furiously.

'I don't see why you should take this attitude. It could have happened to anyone,' she snapped. 'It was only an accident. When I saw the tide was in, I panicked and—and fell!'

'Fell?' He had drawn nearer and now saw the gash in her leg. 'So you've managed to hurt yourself also!' he said unsympathetically. 'Why on earth should you have waited until flood tide? Isa tells me she warned you. If you had set off in time, you would have been able to make your way across the rocks without having this "accident", as you call it!'

'Anyone could have fallen,' she replied sullenly. 'The boulders are slippery.'

But he had pulled out a big handkerchief and was binding it firmly around the wound. 'Why did you not tie something around that cut?' he asked irritably. 'You should have tried to stop the bleeding.'

As he bent down and picked her up as easily as if she weighed no more than a child, she said sharply, 'I can walk quite well, thanks! All I need is a little help!'

He did not answer and she marvelled at how surefootedly he carried her across the jagged, treacherous rocks. He marched along the white strand and deposited her in the boat, with one of his old tweed coats about her shoulders.

As the boat turned back towards Kinneil, he regarded

her thoughtfully from his seat in the stern. 'You haven't told me why you left things so late. Did you forget that Isa had warned you to watch the time? Don't tell me you're one of those romantic dreamy girls who go around making up poetry about the landscape, the beauty of the clouds, and so on!'

'No, I'm not poetic,' she retorted bitterly. 'But now I wish I'd seen more of the Island. As it is, I saw a little house—the black house. Isa told me about it. It was in a dreadful state and I tidied it up. It was stupid of me. I only wish now I'd left it as it was.'

'What!' His voice, powerful at all times, echoed across the waters. 'You mean you have the cheek to tell me you were prowling about the black house? You tidied it up? What business is it of yours how I keep it? Did it not occur to you that I might *like* it untidy? You're a typical female, prying and interfering, and trying to organise a man's life, whether he likes it or not! I hope you didn't have nerve enough to interfere with my specimens?'

'All I did was sweep it, and throw out some of those disgusting tins and rubbish,' she protested angrily. 'And clean out the ashes, and—and fill that horrible old iron kettle at the stream, and——' She choked, feeling herself on the verge of tears.

'Exactly what I thought!' he said grimly. 'Now if you'd been the man who *should* have arrived, it wouldn't have occurred to him to meddle. He would have left things exactly where they were. Don't you realise that people who work outdoors don't have time to worry about all the little fussy details of domestic life? If there's one thing I can't stand it's an interfering woman!'

'It seems to me you don't like women in any shape or form!' she retorted tartly.

A faint smile softened the craggy granite mask of his face. 'I wouldn't go as far as to say that,' he replied.

'Anyway,' she went on, 'I shan't be staying! I'm not any

more anxious for your company than you are for mine. I'll leave by the first boat.'

'Oh no, you won't,' he replied, with his former brusqueness.

Beverley regarded him incredulously. 'What on earth do you mean? Do you really think I'm going to stay on here and be a target for your revolting, horrible manners?'

'Whether you like my manners or not is immaterial,' he replied evenly. 'You certainly won't be able to go far with your leg in that condition. Don't you realise you've got quite a nasty cut? It won't heal up overnight, you know.'

She glanced down and with a feeling of horror saw the dark stain that had spread through his white handkerchief. The excitement of her little adventure, and her passage of arms with Alex Ramage, had put her misery in the background of her mind. But now the wound was throbbing painfully and it was with relief she realised that they had reached Kinneil. This time she made no objection as he carried her towards the guesthouse.

The two Miss MacCrimmons were waiting at the door, Isa's plump face anxious, and Morag looking rather grim.

Isa gave a little gasp as she saw Beverley's bandaged leg. 'My goodness, just what I thought! Didn't I say, Morag, that she might have met with an accident?'

'Yes, yes, you did!' Morag returned irritably.

'I'm afraid I slipped on the rocks,' Beverley said in a small voice. 'I waited too long and then panicked when I saw the tide was in.'

'Poor dear!' Isa said sympathetically. 'Did your watch stop?'

'Oh, I was—was looking around the island,' Beverley replied.

'She means,' Alex broke in, 'that she decided the black house needed a bit of cleaning up.'

'And so it does, I expect,' said Isa, an edge of sharpness in her voice. 'Well, let's not just stand here chattering.

Better get her up to her room, Alex, and we'll get her a nice hot cup of tea and see to that leg.'

When he had swept her upstairs and had deposited her on her bed, he turned to Isa and remarked unflatteringly, 'She looks a bit white about the gills. Perhaps I should ring for Dr MacPhee.'

'I'm perfectly all right!' Beverley told him firmly.

'Oh, I don't think there's any need,' Isa said doubtfully. 'I'll have a look at her leg, but I don't think we'll have to send for him. And just as well, for he can be right bad-tempered if he's called out in the evening.'

For a moment Alex hesitated in uncharacteristic indecision, then nodding curtly, turned and left the room.

Later, as Isa gently bathed the wound, Beverley said wryly, 'It seems to me that on the whole the men on Kinneil are a pretty bad-tempered lot.'

Isa laughed. 'Oh, you mustn't go by Alex. He breaks all the rules. And even he can be charming when he wants.'

'Well, he's certainly not charming to me!' Beverley remarked.

'Take no heed of him,' Isa said soothingly, as she tied the last knot in the bandage. 'Now, there you are! How does that feel?'

'Much better,' Beverley told her gratefully. 'You really have been sweet about everything. I feel such an awful nuisance!'

'Nonsense!' Isa said crisply. 'Morag and I are delighted to have you. Here!' She handed Beverley a glass of water and a couple of tablets. 'These will help you to sleep. But first, Morag is going to bring you up a nice cup of tea, with a couple of her home-made bannocks.' Her stout face broke into a smile. 'I think that's why Morag likes Alex. He's always praising her for her bannocks, and says they're the best in the whole of the Western Isles. But now, I'll away. Morag will be up shortly.'

A little later Morag arrived, deposited a tray on her

bedside table and enquired with gruff kindness if she was feeling better. When she too had gone, Beverley sipped the light fragrant tea, then lay back against the snowy white pillows that smelt faintly of broom, listening to the surge of water as it raced through the narrow channel between the two islands. What a strange and unexpected ending to her first day in the Hebrides, she was thinking. Now, for better or for worse, she would have to remain in this little homely guesthouse for at least some days to come. The prospect would have been delightful, without Alex Ramage's antagonistic presence. Well, at any rate, it was a good thing she would not be working for him! He would have made a horrible employer.

She tried to visualise what it would have been like working on that little isle. Primrose Isle, it should be called, she thought dreamily, because that was how she had first seen it, smothered in a pale yellow haze of primroses. Yes, Primrose Isle. But somehow the name didn't seem suitable as a place for Alex Ramage. Not rugged enough for him!

She drifted off to sleep soothed by the sound of rushing waters and the wild eerie cry of seagulls.

She awoke on the following morning to hear Alex's heavy footsteps descending the stairs. She glanced at her watch. It was early, but already the day had begun for him. He must be very devoted to his work, she thought a little grumpily. At any rate, he didn't seem to realise that a man of his weight could make considerable noise coming down the wooden stairs, unless he took care to step lightly in consideration for the sleeping household. But then he didn't strike her as a particularly considerate person!

During the following days she was to become accustomed to those heavy footsteps and to the sound of his deep voice when he returned in the evenings. She used to strain her ears to catch the words, then would become cross with herself for bothering to listen. After all, what did it matter what the man was saying? He was an unutterable boor, and the less she heard of him the better!

Sometimes, however, he stayed on the isle overnight. Then, strangely enough, she missed the sound of his footsteps passing her door in the mornings and the put-put of the outboard motor as he returned in the evening. What important business could be delaying him there? she wondered. Certainly not the beauty of that enchanting, flower-smothered island, with its graceful silver birches and its cool sparkling burns that gushed over the white quartz stones. What did he think of at night, she wondered, as he sat beside the fire in the centre of the black house? What was his history? Well, that was something she would never discover, because her leg was healing nicely, and soon she would be leaving Kinneil for ever.

Life at the guesthouse proved to be very comfortable. Morag was an excellent cook and showed her innate kindness by serving up the most delicious meals; salmon from the local rivers with home-made mayonnaise and a salad; cherries and cream to follow; buttery shortbreads for tea and a glass of delicious frothy buttermilk with her meals. At first Beverley had been doubtful whether she would enjoy buttermilk, but Isa had persuaded her, and she had found it delicious; crisp and astringent and refreshing. But then everything on Kinneil was enchanting, she decided. Even the cream had a fragrant taste and smell.

She mentioned this to Isa one day when she had been promoted to sit in the parlour with her leg up on a cushioned chair. 'It's true,' Isa agreed, 'you see, so many wildflowers grow here. The cows eat these, and the milk, as a result, is perfumed.' She laughed. 'In fact, visitors tell me that the very breath of the cows is scented on Kinneil.'

'Kinneil seems to be a beautiful place,' Beverley said regretfully. 'How I should have loved to have seen it, and explored every nook and cranny!'

Gradually her leg healed and she was able to make her way to a lounge hammock in the garden where she stretched out comfortably in its wide swinging seat beneath the fringed canopy. Here the air was full of scents from the wide herbaceous border where Isa worked magic amongst the flowers with knowledgeable fingers. Watching her, Beverley could well understand how the garden was in such a flourishing condition, for it was plain that Isa's plump little fingers held the secret of making things grow. Never outside the pages of an illustrated storybook had Beverley seen such a profusion of blossoms.

She said this to Isa one morning when she came to sit by her in a camp-chair, pulling off the battered old panama hat she usually wore in the garden, and fanning her hot face with it.

'I think it's the loveliest garden I've ever seen,' Beverley told her enthusiastically.

Isa smiled. 'Oh, I think some of the credit must go to the wonderful Gulf Stream. You can grow lots of plants in the Hebrides that wouldn't flourish anywhere else in Britain. My father was a sea-captain, and he brought back plants from all parts of the world. But our garden is not a patch on the Redferns' garden at Kinneil Castle. It makes me quite envious. But then Lynne Redfern's people have so much money they can do anything they like. The gardens are beautifully kept with plants from the glasshouses, so that they can change them whenever they show the first signs of fading. And then they have a wonderful herb garden with every sort of herb you can imagine.'

'Lynne Redfern,' murmured Beverley. 'The name sounds English.'

'Oh, they are an English family,' Isa told her, 'but while they're here on Kinneil they're more Scottish than the Scots themselves. They always hold a ball on Lynne's birthday, when the men wear the kilt and many of the ladies appear in white dresses, wearing a sash of an appropriate tartan.'

'An appropriate tartan?' queried Beverley.

Isa's round blue eyes twinkled in her plump face. 'It's one way of saying that if you've no right to wear any particular tartan, you may choose the pattern that most takes your fancy. Some of the visitors look most peculiar in the kilt, I can tell you, and you see some comical sights. But if ever there was a man born to wear the kilt it's Alex Ramage!'

'Somehow it's hard to imagine him relaxing at a ball,' Beverley said dryly.

'Oh, *everyone* goes,' said Isa. 'It's a pity you couldn't have stayed on. Lynne's birthday's on the tenth of next month and I know you'd have enjoyed your first experience of a Scottish ball. In a way it's a lucky thing for us Lynne fell for Alex, otherwise I don't think they'd have come back this year, in spite of everything.'

'In spite of everything?'

'Yes, in spite of the terrible fiasco when Lynne tried to be Alex's assistant. It didn't work out at all well, and must have put Alex off the idea of ever having a woman assistant again.'

'You mean that Lynne Redfern was Alex's assistant?' Beverley asked in surprise.

'Yes, for a little while. I expect she thought it would be a good excuse to be near him and to be in his company as much as possible. But she was much too spoiled and cosseted to endure the hardships of the life and the endless hard work. They had a frightful quarrel and off she went in a huff! The next thing I heard of her was that she was at a big reception in London where royalty was present. I saw it in a gossip magazine one of our guests brought here. All the same, she came back to Kinneil later that summer and they made it up. But he won't as much as allow her to visit him on Solan. She chatters too much and interferes with his plans. And that's something he won't put up with—not even from Lynne, lovely as she is! The pity is that she's to blame for his refusing to have a woman assistant. He thinks they'd all be the same as Lynne—hopelessly spoiled, and sulking if things don't go their own way.'

'I see,' Beverley said slowly. 'So that's why he wouldn't even give me a trial! After all, he might have guessed that when I had travelled all this way I was really keen. Well, it just wasn't to be! My leg's practically cured now and I'll have to go home.'

'Stay on for a while!' Isa urged. 'It's early in the season, and we've loads of room.'

Beverley laughed ruefully. 'I only wish I could! There's nothing I'd like better, but it's something that simply can't be managed. I can't live on air. And I certainly wouldn't allow you to keep me for nothing.'

CHAPTER THREE

A FEW evenings later, making the excuse that she felt tired, Beverley went up to her room early.

But she did not go to bed right away. Instead, she busied herself with packing, for she had decided to leave on the following day. Her leg had healed and now she had no excuse for staying on any longer. To do so would be to impose on the generosity of the MacCrimmon sisters.

She felt depressed as she moved quietly about her room, putting her things into her suitcases. In the morning she would be gone from the place for ever. Her dream was at an end. And what a hare-brained scheme hers had been! She had been a fool to throw away her secure job in the hope of finding a new way of life here in the Hebrides. It had all come to nothing. Serve you right! no doubt her family would tell her when she returned, defeated. After all, they had warned her not to persist in her deception, but she had forged ahead regardless of consequences.

As twilight made the room shadowy, she lit the rosy-shaded lamp by her bedside, undressed and got into bed. And as she picked up the last of her paperbacks with its pretty, attractive cover, she was thinking that this was the last night she would spend in this dainty, old-fashioned room. In the morning she would break it to the sisters that she had made up her mind to leave when the ferry sailed from Kinneil. She had also made up her mind that as soon as she got home she would send them a sizeable sum from her savings. After that, it would be up to her to look around for another job.

As she read, her depression was forgotten and it was later than she had intended when at last, yawning sleepily, she stretched out her hand to turn out the lamp.

As she did so she heard Alex's deep voice resound through the house.

How little they had seen of each other since that fatal first day on Solan which had ended so disastrously! Beverley had made every effort to avoid him, waiting until he was safely out of the house in the mornings before making her way downstairs. In the evenings too, she had gone to her room early and had read, often late into the night. There had, of course, been short meetings, when they had been coldly polite to each other.

It was strange to think that on the following day she would be gone for ever, and would never see him again. Stranger still to think that she would miss the sound of his heavy footsteps ascending the wooden stairs in the evening.

But this evening was to be different!

Instead of his steps continuing upwards past her door, there was a pause and a sharp rap on the panels.

For a moment she gazed at the door fixedly, wondering if in some magical way he had guessed that this was to be

her last night on Kinneil, and had come to wish her
goodbye and good fortune.

She called 'Come in', and as his bulk appeared in the
doorway she saw how he lowered his head as he entered—
the automatic action of a man who had learned by bitter
experience that the lintels of many doors were often just a
little too low.

Without speaking, he pulled up a chair, seated himself,
and gazed at her frowningly, then said abruptly, 'You seem
to be avoiding me. Why?'

For a moment she was taken aback by the unexpectedness of the question, then she retorted angrily,
'Why shouldn't I? Isn't that what you want?'

He did not reply to this. Instead, he asked, 'What made
you think of coming here anyway? It was not the sort of job
that would have appealed to most girls.'

'Perhaps I'm not like "most girls",' she snapped. 'It just
so happens that I always wanted to see the Hebrides. My
mother came from Skye, and she used to tell me about it,
and about the wonderful opalescent colours of the sky and
on the sea. Apart from that, I've always loved being outdoors, and the idea of working with animals appealed to
me.'

'And what were you doing before you got this idea into
your head?'

She hesitated. 'I—I worked in an insurance office,' she
told him lamely.

A faint smile crossed his face. 'That doesn't sound very
much like outdoor work.'

'No, it certainly wasn't,' she agreed wryly. 'And I always
hated it. When I saw your advertisement, it was like the
answer to my dream. It meant I could see the Hebrides
and, at the same time, earn my living. I thought that if I
made a success of it, perhaps I could take on this sort of job
permanently.'

'Now that's ridiculous!' he told her tersely. 'Wildcats

look very much like tabby cats, but they're savage and untamable. Stags can savage a human being. This is not a pets' corner at the zoo, you know!'

'I know that perfectly well,' she retorted indignantly.

'Anyway, that's not what I want to speak to you about,' he went on, ignoring her annoyance. 'I've been thinking things over about the black house. It's true, I was a bit annoyed at first when I saw what you had done to it, but I must admit it's a lot more comfortable, and I've decided I've no objection to taking on someone to take care of it. At present, I'm concentrating on the marine life of Solan, which will give me more than enough to do, so I'm asking you to stay on. Not as my assistant, mark you, but as my girl Friday——'

'You mean, as your dogsbody,' she interposed indignantly.

'You can put it any way you like,' he replied. 'But I've made it clear to you just what I want you to do. You can come on those terms, or not at all. It's up to you.'

Beverley drew a deep breath. She was on the point of telling him exactly what she thought of such a proposition, when he stood up, spun the chair into the corner of the room with a deft twist of the wrist, and with a crisp, 'Think it over!' walked out.

When he had gone, and Beverley had simmered down sufficiently to think clearly, it struck her that she had the choice of returning home defeated, and letting her family know that all her high hopes had come to nothing, or of remaining on his terms.

Alex Ramage would undoubtedly prove a hard task-master. On the other hand, perhaps she might get the opportunity of proving to him that she was capable of doing more than keeping the black house in order. Yes, she would stay on, she decided.

But she mustn't appear too eager. She would not give him the satisfaction of knowing that she was falling in so easily with his plan.

Her last thought, as she fell asleep, was that it was a good thing she had not told the sisters she intended to leave on the following day. Now they need never know she had changed her mind. All she had to do was quietly to unpack her things in the morning.

The following evening found her riffling through the books on the rather dusty shelves in the parlour, in search of something to read. It was easy to see the MacCrimmon sisters were not bookworms, for the reading available was rather ancient, and it was clear that some of the books had lain on the shelves for years untouched.

With a sigh she replaced a work on the history and structure of sailing ships. The illustrations were speckled brown from age, and smelt of mildew. Obviously this had once belonged to the late Captain MacCrimmon. Then, by chance, she pulled out the book beside it. It looked equally ancient, and she opened it without much enthusiasm. But as she dipped in, scanning here and there, she soon became enthralled.

Still reading, she returned to her favourite armchair, propped the cushions behind her, and settled herself comfortably. For this was the history of the Lords of the Isles. She read how at one time the people of the Western Isles had lived in terror of a tyrant called Godred, who ruled from the Isle of Man. He was of Norwegian descent and his power lay in his fleet of Norwegian longships with their prows carved in the shape of a dragon. But the people found a champion. He was a man with a strange name, Somerled, which meant Summer Voyager, and he was married to Godred's sister. Gradually he built up a fleet of small, very fast ships, keeping them hidden for as long as possible in a bay in the south of the Island of Islay.

But eventually Godred got word of the preparations his brother-in-law was making, and sallied out from the Isle of Man, his fleet of longships moved swiftly over the seas, with their great square sails, the war pennants fluttering at the mastheads, the round, painted shields of the warriors hanging along the sides.

It was a day in January when the two fleets met off the western coast of Islay. All day long the great sea-battle raged, but eventually the small fast ships of Somerled triumphed. Godred was forced to give up some of his power to Somerled, who made his headquarters on Islay. And it was from that beautiful island that the Lords of the Isles ruled over the Hebrides.

Beverley was absorbed in the story, unaware of everything around her, when without warning a hand firmly removed the book from her grasp and, startled, she found herself looking up into the piercing eyes of Alex Ramage.

'So at last you've condescended to join us!' he said dryly. 'What's this? Not another romance, is it? One of the Victorian kind, I suppose, with a wronged heroine and a villain who twirls his moustaches?'

'You needn't sound so superior,' she said tartly. 'And it so happens this is a book about the Hebrides. It's about the Lords of the Isles, and how Somerled defeated his brother-in-law with his fleet of little ships.'

'I suppose it doesn't tell you whether Somerled was a handsome godlike person?' he asked as he sank into an armchair opposite her and with slow deliberate movements began to fill his pipe.

'No, it doesn't,' she told him defensively. 'And even if he was it wouldn't interest me in the slightest. I don't happen to like handsome men. I find plain men more interesting.'

As she saw the faint gleam of amusement in Alex's rugged face, she realised that he could easily take this remark as aimed at him, and said quickly, 'I felt sorry for his wife, though.'

He puffed thoughtfully. 'Why, may I ask?'

'Well, after all, Godred was her brother. They must have grown up together. It must have been horrible for her to realise that he had been defeated by her own husband.'

'You seem to have been giving this matter some thought,' he said. 'It looks as if I'm going to have some complications on my hands when you come across to Solan. Are you going to be the kind of girl who insists on stopping off for discussions on everything that crops up?'

'I haven't said I'm going to take on the job!' she told him swiftly. How typical of the man's arrogance to assume she would immediately fall in with his plans!

'I see. So you're turning me down, is that it?' he asked equably.

Beverley felt faintly piqued that he showed no disappointment. 'Well, no, I didn't mean that either,' she stumbled, realising she was placing herself in a ridiculous position.

'It's as well Somerled wasn't as indecisive as you,' he remarked dryly, 'or he would certainly have lost the battle. I think you'd better let me have a straight yes or no. Stop beating about the bush! Are you or are you not going to take the job?'

'Oh, very well!' she said ungraciously, bridling at the abrupt way he was demanding a decision. 'I don't seem to have any other choice. I don't imagine there are many suitable jobs available on Kinneil.'

He nodded. 'Exactly! And I'm glad to see you're sensible enough not to keep me in suspense. There was always the chance that when you did decide, I might have changed my mind. And now that that little matter is cleared up, you'd better come over to Solan first thing in the morning. By the way, I've spoken to Morag and Isa and they said that, if you were staying, they'd agree to lend a few bits and pieces for the black house, to make it suitable for feminine occupation.'

'There's no need to do me any favours!' she told him indignantly. 'I'm used to roughing it.'

'I'd be interested to know what you consider "roughing

it"?' he enquired. 'I expect you're thinking of camping holidays, and how you enjoyed yourself frying sausages over a barbecue!'

This was so true that Beverley bit back a sharp retort.

'But to get back to it,' he continued, 'Morag has given us permission to root around in the attic and take away anything that catches our fancy, so I suggest we get down to it right away. Well, are you coming?'

He stood up as he spoke and, much to her surprise, Beverley soon found herself meekly climbing the short flight of steps into the dusty attic of Kinneil Guesthouse.

She took a certain amount of pleasure in the fact that while she could stand upright with ease, Alex looked extremely uncomfortable, his head bent down to avoid striking it against the sloping rafters. He was forced to seat himself upon an old brassbound trunk and leave the search to her.

'Very well, fire ahead,' he instructed her. 'Look around and pick out anything you think would do for the house, and I promise you I'll raise no objections.'

She gazed about eagerly and immediately her eye was attracted by an old Victorian crimson plush-covered armchair. There was also a broad roll of linoleum in excellent condition. Immediately she coveted it for the black house, then remembered that the fire was in the centre of the floor. 'I'm afraid we won't be able to take this,' she said regretfully, 'although it would certainly improve the house no end. What a pity the fire is in the middle of the room.'

'Take it anyway,' he told her. 'One of these days, when I'm not too busy, I may get time to make a proper fireplace.'

'Do you really mean that?' she asked doubtfully.

'Of course! With Alex Ramage, his word is his bond!'

For the first time she noticed a hint of humour in his manner, and looked at him curiously. Yes, those stony eyes beneath the thick brows actually held a slight twinkle.

'Well, in that case, we'll take it, just on the offchance that you really mean what you say,' she told him severely.

She also selected a small mahogany table and some chairs. They were a bit scarred, but she knew that if she polished them carefully they would come up quite nicely.

There was also a tea-chest full of odds and ends of china—cups, plates, saucers, and tureens—remnants, no doubt, of cherished tea and dinner services, beautifully designed and of bone china.

Later, Alex helped her to unearth, under a pile of junk, a lovely old farmhouse dresser. It would be just perfect for storing cutlery and her odds and ends of crockery, she decided, already visualising how pretty those gleaming pieces of bone china would look on display.

Beverley found her search becoming more and more like a treasure-hunt. Alex, who had resumed his seat on the trunk, surveyed her in silence, puffing at his pipe, while she rummaged and exclaimed excitedly as she added to her store.

But at last came the moment when he reneged on his promise not to interfere. It was when she came upon a large folding draught-screen studded with shells of every shape and colour from palest lemon to transparent pearly pink. It must have been the handiwork of some long gone Mac-Crimmon woman, who had diligently gathered these shells on the platinum-white beachs of the islands. 'Oh, we must have this!' she exclaimed with delight.

'No, I'm afraid that's *out*,' Alex said firmly.

'What do you mean?' she asked indignantly. 'You said you wouldn't raise any objections.'

'But we don't need it,' he told her. 'In the black house it's not necessary to keep the draughts out. It's fully insulated. You see, those ancestors of ours knew all about building with cavity walls. They made two separate walls of stone and filled the space between them with earth, or sometimes with peat. They were designed to afford protection against storms, and did their job very satisfactorily, so black houses are very cosy, although they may look bleak. Anyway, that screen's enormous. It would take up too much room.'

'You've gone back on your promise,' Beverley reminded him stubbornly.

'Well, I didn't foresee you'd set your heart on a thing like this,' he replied irritably. 'It's the kind of fussy, silly thing a woman would like.'

'You don't think much of women, do you?' she retorted angrily. 'Anyway, *I'd* like to have it!'

'You don't seem to realise that everything will have to be taken to Solan by boat, or carted across the sand when the tide is out. But don't let that influence you. Take it by all means, if you wish, but you can transport it yourself! On those conditions you're quite welcome to it.'

It might have blown up into a full-scale quarrel, but luckily Beverley's attention was diverted as she reached into an open tin box and discovered a package of old letters. Eagerly she fingered them. Letters from the past were like windows opening into the life of someone else, with all its joys and sorrows and adventures. Perhaps these belonged to the same girl who had made the beautiful shell screen.

There were other packages in the box, some tied with tape, others just jumbled together. She had an inkling of what she would find—old faded recipes, and household account books, written in watery brownish ink.

She was about to draw Alex's attention to the letters, but he had already dipped into the box and was absorbed in an old newspaper of a bygone day. Huffily, Beverley decided not to be the first to reopen the conversation.

Leaving the tin box aside for the moment, she opened an ancient leather-covered square trunk, its corners reinforced with brass, and drew in her breath in delight as she saw what lay on top—a length of the most exquisite silk she had ever seen. It had a raised pattern of tiny pagodas against an ivory-white background. Carefully she lifted it out and noticed how in the slight draught of air from the open door, the threads in an edge of the material fluffed out and shimmered.

Lower down in the trunk she found a white dress in an old-world style, slightly yellowed now, it was plain this was a cherished wedding-gown. With it was a wide veil of hand-made lace.

It also contained more up-to-date fabrics, remnants of cotton and chintz and cheerful large-patterned cretonnes, and a piece of vivid red terry towelling, which she instantly earmarked for curtain material. It would make a bright splash of colour in the dimness of the black house. She would have to ask permission, of course, but she felt so sure of obtaining it that she picked the bright cloth out of the box and placed it with the items she had already selected.

Alex folded the newspaper and replaced it in the box, then dipped in again and drew out a Valentine with a lacy border. In the centre was a satin heart pierced by a silver arrow.

'To let you know my heart is true,
I send this Valentine to you.'

read Beverley, as he handed it to her. 'It's lovely, isn't it, but sad too. I wonder what happened, and if they married and lived happily ever after.'

Alex regarded it without enthusiasm. 'Can't imagine how anyone could waste their time and their bawbees on rubbish like this!' he remarked squashingly.

'Well, I think it's romantic!' she insisted. 'I don't really think there's *anything* you approve of, Mr Ramage.'

'Let's cut out the "Mr Ramage" now that we're working together,' he instructed. 'And you're wrong, you know. There's one thing I would give my full approval to, and that's a cup of Morag's hot strong tea. I'm getting a bit tired of old attics and their dusty mementoes.' He got to his feet and stretched his arms wide, remembering just in time to stoop where the rafters sloped.

Serve him right if he had knocked his head! Beverley thought crossly. There was nothing she would have liked better than to remain in the attic, going through the contents of the box at her leisure. Reluctantly she replaced the Valentine, and closed the lid.

'You've collected quite a pile of loot,' Alex remarked, surveying the items they had laid aside. 'More than I expected. It will take some time to get this downstairs, so I'd better make a start.' As he spoke he lifted the armchair as lightly as if it weighed no more than a feather, and eased it out of the attic.

Later that evening, when everything had been stored in an outbuilding, and they had had tea accompanied by some of Morag's bannocks with honey, Beverley stole out of the house for a peep, hoping against hope that he had relented and had brought down the shell draught-screen. But no, it was not there. She felt a pang of disappointment, and then told herself what a fool she was to have imagined for a moment that a man as inflexible as Alex Ramage would have changed his mind and decided to humour her.

Her shoulders drooping, she went back to the house to show the length of red towelling to the sisters, and to ask if she might have it for curtains for the black house.

Almost in unison, they agreed.

Isa smiled. 'You know, that's been up there for the past couple of years. I got it in a remnant sale on the mainland. I always meant to do something with it, but never got around to it. I'm glad it's going to be useful at last.'

Curious about the exquisite piece of silk, Beverley questioned the sisters about it.

'Yes, it is beautiful, isn't it? One doesn't see the like nowadays. Our father brought it back from Bangkok,' Isa told her.

Beverley was awake early next morning, too excited to sleep at the thought of beginning her new career. But, early as it was, when she went downstairs the MacCrimmon sisters were already up.

Morag was standing at the kitchen table which was covered with tinned foods and other necessary things to be taken to Solan. She looked up as Beverley came in, her hard bony features relaxing into a smile. 'Well, I must say I'm glad you and Alex have hit it off at last!' she said.

'I don't know about that,' Beverley replied doubtfully. 'All that's happened is that he's decided to take on someone to take care of the black house, and thinks I'll do as well as anyone else.'

'The poor creature can't cook,' Morag remarked. 'When he stays on Solan for the day I pity him, because usually he just keeps on working and doesn't stop, not even to boil an egg. Well, now at least he'll be properly taken care of, and get his meals regularly. By the way, I've two dozen eggs in that cardboard box, so be careful of them, and I'll get you more as you need them. I've also looked out some tins of food. You can take them over with you this morning.'

Beverley looked at the selection in some surprise. It included tins of haggis and cock-a-leekie soup, made by a famous Scottish firm, also crab and prawns and mushrooms, and even a tinned Dundee cake.

Isa joined them at the table, saying with some asperity, 'Really, Morag, you spoil that man! These are not the sort of rations Beverley should be taking with her! Baked beans and some pease meal would be more like it!'

'Ah well, I think a man needs a treat now and again,' Morag replied. 'And Alex has a sweet tooth, as we all know.'

'He may have a sweet tooth,' Beverley put in, siding with Isa, 'but he certainly hasn't a sweet manner.'

'It's true, he can be difficult at times,' Morag agreed, 'but he really forgets everything when he's at work. He may be too forthright, I admit, but he's straight and honest and speaks his mind. There's nothing of the hypocrite about him. And that's the sort of man I like!'

'Maybe so,' Isa allowed reluctantly, 'but one can be *too* outspoken. I think being a bit more polite wouldn't do him any harm.'

Beverley listened as the sisters wrangled amicably while they packed a large wooden box. And when it was ready she helped Morag to carry it down to the jetty, where Alex was busy loading a boat with some of the items she had picked out on the previous evening. On top, firmly lashed down, was the red plush chair. There was also something new here which she was very pleased to see, a camp cooker with four jets, and complete with a couple of cylinders of bottled gas.

When Morag had returned to the house, Alex opened the box and turned the tins over in his hand. 'Crab! Lobster! What would we be doing with things like that on Solan? I don't want fancy food, and I don't want fancy cooking either. Tatties and a tin of beans will do nicely.'

'There's not much point in employing me if you don't want anything better than that,' Beverley told him severely, as she gingerly stepped on board the laden boat. 'Well, I'm determined to see you get your money's worth. But you needn't worry. I'm not a particularly good cook, so you won't be getting anything too elaborate. Anyway,' she added, 'Morag tells me you have a sweet tooth.'

She glanced at him as she said this and to her satisfaction thought she saw a faint look of embarrassment cross his face, then decided she had only imagined it.

'This is your place!' he indicated the armchair.

For an instant she was about to protest, then thought better of it and, without a word, seated herself, very conscious that she must present a comic picture floating out to Solan enthroned in a red plush Victorian armchair.

CHAPTER FOUR

WHEN they arrived Alex untied the armchair and marched off with it to the black house, Beverley trailing behind with some of the lighter articles.

They spent the morning getting the house in order. Alex removed all signs of the central fire and laid the linoleum, while Beverley busied herself at the new camp cooker. It was small and light, but she was delighted to find that it worked very efficiently.

Time sped by as she discovered a hundred and one things to be done. She fetched water in the great iron kettle, heated it on the cooker, and scrubbed the tiny window clean of encrusted dust and the accumulation of cobwebs of years. When she was finished, she stood back and observed with satisfaction how the bright, opalescent Hebridean light brightened up the black house as it filtered through the newly cleaned window.

In spite of Alex's boasted preference for beans and tatties, Beverley noticed smugly that he appeared to enjoy the stew she had put on to simmer while they got on with the chores.

'Not bad!' he pronounced, when he had tasted it. 'I think you underestimate yourself when you say you're not a good cook.'

She laughed. 'Oh, anyone can make a stew! It's the simplest thing in the world.'

He shook his head. 'I don't know about that! It seems to me that with an accomplishment like this you could get almost any man you fancied on Kinneil.'

Beverley found herself flushing a little with annoyance.

'I didn't come here husband-hunting,' she told him stiffly.

'I don't say you did! All I'm remarking is that you'd make a very suitable wife for an islandman—that's of course if you intended to settle here.'

'I haven't looked that far ahead,' she told him. 'Anyway, I'm not thinking of marriage—not at present, at any rate.'

'That's what all girls say!' he replied. 'But it's amazing how swiftly they marry when they get the opportunity.'

Beverley got to her feet and swept up the plates. How typical of the man—just when she had thought that he was becoming comparatively civil, he spoilt everything by remarks like these! 'I think it's time we got back to work,' she said tightly.

'What? You mean, there's to be no afters?' He got to his feet with a sigh. 'Very well, I suppose we'd better get on with it. Although we'll have to take over a few more boat-loads before things are in order.'

As the days passed the little house took shape and she could pause to survey it with pleasure, thinking how attractive it was. Alex had brought over the dresser and she had arranged the odd pieces of china on it. And now there was a proper table, the mahogany beginning to gleam again, for she had polished it well. The chairs were odd, of course, but still one was now able to sit down to a meal in the middle of the day.

She held the towelling material against the window, the scarlet a vivid splash against the stone walls. She would run up curtains that very night on the little hand-sewing machine belonging to the MacCrimmons, for she felt sure they would permit her to use it.

'My, you are a little home-maker, aren't you?' Alex's voice spoke behind her.

Instantly she was on the defensive. 'So you're satisfied, are you?' she snapped. 'You weren't so pleased when I tidied it up the first time I came here.'

'I know better now,' he admitted. 'And in all sincerity I say you've done a marvellous job.'

Beverley, in spite of herself, felt a glow of satisfaction at his words.

But it was shortlived, for the very next day disaster struck. And it came about in the simplest way possible.

They had started out very early, and by mid-morning Beverley was more than ready for a refreshing cup of tea. She picked up the big black iron kettle. It had been designed for use over a peat fire, and was heavy even when empty. She filled it at a point where the fast-flowing burn leaped over a little ledge of rock, forming a miniature waterfall, and as she turned to retrace her steps it swung around in her hands, sending a stream of icy water over her stockings and light canvas shoes.

As she returned to the black house she caught a glimpse of Alex stooping over the pools amidst the boulders that stretched out in rocky arms into the sea. He was completely engrossed, she realised, and as she squelched back to the black house she was in anything but a good temper.

The ancient kettle was so large that it took up two rings on the cooker and she was forced to take off a pot in which she was steaming a pudding for lunch.

As soon as the kettle began to boil, she went out to hail Alex. For an instant, he turned his head in her direction, waved in an absentminded sort of way, then, his attention on something in the sand-dunes, he moved back swiftly over the slippery boulders. For a moment Beverley was tempted to discover what it was that had caught his notice, but there was a chilly breeze blowing, and her feet felt icy cold and wet in her damp canvas shoes, and she decided she would return to the house for a hot cup of tea. She would not wait for him. If he wanted to drink cold tea— well, that was his own business, she thought with exasperation.

As she had guessed, it was some time before he made his appearance. And when he did arrive it was evident that he too was in a bad humour. He pulled out a chair and sat down without speaking, then waited in oppressive silence while she poured tea for him.

'Will you have a sandwich?' Beverley ventured at last, disconcerted by his continued silence.

He put down his cup with a sudden crash. 'I wonder if you know that by yelling at me like that you have lost me a grayling, a very rare specimen on Solan, by the way.'

She looked at him in astonishment. 'But I don't even know what a grayling is——' she began.

'A butterfly,' he informed her. '*Hipparchia semele,* if you want to be precise. It has been seen on the shores of Iona, but one doesn't expect to see it here on Solan.'

Beverley felt her blood boil. So it was his precious butterfly that had put him in the sulks. 'I'm *so* sorry,' she said, with heavy sarcasm. '*Do* forgive me for calling you. I didn't realise how important it was to you.'

He regarded her with faint surprise. 'Hello, what's the matter with you? You sound quite ratty.'

'I suppose *you're* the only one who's allowed to be ratty!' she returned sharply. 'Look!' She pointed to her stockings and shoes. 'I'm simply soaked! And it's the fault of that old iron kettle. It's much too heavy when it's full. And what's more, I had to take off the pudding, and it shouldn't have come off the boil—but of course, I wouldn't expect you to know that! The only thing you know about is graylings, and spiders and—and——' She stopped, speechless with anger.

Alex looked at her unsympathetically. 'You seem to have been having a trying morning! But remember, when you called me I lost sight of the grayling and after all, this is my business in life! Do you really consider your problems with an old iron kettle more important than the loss of a unique specimen?'

'Well, after all, you did employ me to take care of the domestic side of things,' she pointed out tightly.

'Not to the extent of interrupting my work!' he retorted.

'Perhaps then I'd better not call you in for tea,' she found her voice rising shrilly.

'Suit yourself! After all, this morning tea business was your idea in the first place.'

She suddenly found herself blazingly angry. 'Why, I don't care if you never——' Words choked her. 'Well, *I* intend to have my tea! And what's more, I'm not going to use that horrible old kettle again. I want a light handy one! And I want it this very day!'

'What you do is your own business!' he told her brusquely. 'But don't let's have any more of this ridiculous business! It's beginning to become rather a bore.'

He stood up and was on the point of stalking from the room when, to her horror, Beverley found herself saying hotly, 'I'm not surprised Lynne Redfern chucked up her job with you. You're the most arrogant, self-opinionated——'

Before she could conclude her sentence he swung around, his eyes blazing. 'So you've been listening to the village gossip, is that it? Well, just remember this, your business is to attend to the house, nothing more or less, and I'll be pleased to be spared your opinion of my private life!'

And, before she could recover from this assault, he strode from the room.

For a moment she stood, her hands clutched, tense with rage. Then she dashed the dishes into the plastic basin and began the washing-up, her mind furiously going over ways and means as to how she could carry out her threat of obtaining a new kettle by hook or by crook. It wasn't really the kettle, she told herself, a little ruefully when she had simmered down a little. It was simply the principle of the thing! She was determined to show Alex Ramage that he couldn't ride roughshod over her.

When she had dried up and tidied away, she considered the possibilities more calmly. She could easily manage the boat, she thought. She had watched Alex, and it seemed easily manoeuvrable.

Everything seemed to favour her plan.

When she was ready to leave she scoured the surround-

ing countryside with a pair of powerful binoculars that
Alex kept hanging behind the door. There was no sign of
him. He was probably on the other side of the island, she
decided with satisfaction, well out of sight of the house.

Gathering up her raincoat and handbag, she ran down
to the beach. She left her belongings on the dry silvery
sands of the dunes while she pushed the light boat into the
water.

It took her only a moment or two to retrieve her posses-
sions from the sand-dunes, but as she turned back towards
the boat she stood in open-mouthed horror as she saw that
it was drifting out to sea, and was every moment gathering
speed as it bobbed farther and farther out of reach. Too late,
she remembered all she had been told of the mysterious
currents in the waters around the little island. And now she
was horror-stricken by the thought of what Alex would feel
when, his day's work on Solan finished, he looked about for
the boat to take them back to Kinneil. She simply daren't
tell him she had let it drift away to sea. Somehow or other
she must get it back before he returned to the black house.

Luckily she was a good swimmer. She kicked off her
canvas shoes and plunged into the water in her cotton
dress. In her excitement, she barely noticed the coldness of
the water. The boat was taking a curious path, weaving
round the island rather than floating out to sea, and she
swam after it as fast as she could. But, in spite of all her
efforts, she found it impossible to close the gap, for the boat
was drifting faster and faster.

After a while she realised with terror that she was becoming overtaken by fatigue. She had no idea how long she
had been swimming, but now she was hazily aware that she
could see around the point of the island and, to her relief,
she caught sight of Alex. Wearing waders, he was standing
on a spit of rock that jutted into the sea, but his back was
towards her, as he examined the pools. Beverley tried to cry
out and attract his attention, but her breath was carried

away by the breeze. As though in a dream she felt herself being dragged closer and closer to those jagged menacing rocks.

She was just about to give up, and allow herself the luxury of sinking down, down into the waters, when she felt herself being grasped and hauled upwards.

She remembered nothing more until she came to in the black house, and found herself leaning back on the red plush chair. She struggled to get up, water streaming from her hair. 'The boat,' she gasped. 'It's drifted away; I must get it.'

The hand that pushed her back into the chair was surprisingly gentle. 'Take it easy! The currents around Solan have their own way of bringing back what the sea takes. It will end up in one of the little bays on the other side of the island, you'll see. It will be waiting for us there, when we go in search of it—a bit the worse for wear, perhaps, but no doubt seaworthy.'

Beverley gazed at him, her eyes wide. Surely this man with the soft reassuring words couldn't be the brusque Alex Ramage to whom she had become accustomed! Weakened by her ordeal, she felt tears prick her eyes. In a way, it would have been easier had he been angry and reproachful; that would have been something she could resent and be on the defensive about.

But somehow this unusual gentleness completely disarmed her and made her feel even more guilty concerning the loss of the boat.

She felt a cup of tea being placed in her hand. 'Here, take this! It will buck you up, and in no time you will be your usual spitfire self.'

'Spitfire?' she quavered. 'I don't feel at all like a spitfire.'

He gave a sudden smile that made him surprisingly boyish-looking. 'Not now, perhaps, but presently you'll be back on form, I assure you.' The tea was too hot and very black, but obediently she sipped it. Did he really consider her a spitfire? Was that how she appeared to him, when all she had been trying to do was to hold her own against his aggressive manner?

'And now, if you feel sufficiently recovered, may I ask what happened?' he asked. 'It was lucky for you I chanced to look around in the nick of time, and there you were, floating towards me like a bit of flotsam. I had barely time to grab you before you got dashed against the rocks.'

Beverley bit her lip. Flotsam indeed! She was feeling all sorts of a fool, but she managed to falter out an explanation.

He looked at her in astonishment. 'I see! So you took the boat and set off for a kettle! Really, you are a confounded little idiot, aren't you, Beverley!'

But this was too much! 'It was all your fault!' she blazed. 'I spoke to you about the kettle and you dared me——'

'Dared you?' he broke in.

'Well, that's how I looked on it,' she told him, a little lamely.

'Look, Beverley,' he said in quiet reasonable tones, 'you risked losing the boat. Nothing can excuse it. Boats like that don't grow on trees, you know.'

'I didn't mean to lose the wretched thing,' she protested. 'I saw how easy it was to handle and I was perfectly sure I could manage——' Her voice faltered into silence.

'Well, it's fairly obvious now that you *don't* know how to handle it,' he told her dryly. 'But let's say no more about it. I'll see if it's drifted in yet. I'd better get you back to Kinneil before you catch your death of cold in those wet clothes.

When he went out, Beverley got to her feet and, as she towelled her hair dry and ran a comb through it, her fighting spirit came to life again. Alex Ramage was an impossible person to deal with, she told herself. Serve him right if he had to scour the beaches of the Island for the boat! When he came back, she would be careful to show no further signs of regret for what had happened.

During the next few days, Beverley did manage to get a bright new kettle from MacKenzie's general shop, and also to borrow a cookery book from the MacCrimmon sisters. She began to experiment with different dishes, although she was careful not to produce anything that Alex could contemptuously describe as 'fancy'.

Then one morning she awoke to the realisation that today was her birthday.

Isa came in with morning tea, drew back the curtains, and let the shimmering opalescent light into her room. Beside the toast-rack was a pile of envelopes having the stiff outlines that could only mean birthday cards. Beverley pounced on them with delight and, watched by the smiling Isa, quickly opened them. There were cards from her father and mother, and even one from her brother in Saudi Arabia, apart from an assortment from relatives and friends.

'Take your tea before it gets cold,' Isa urged. But she lingered, and Beverley guessed that she was curious.

'It's my birthday,' she exclaimed, 'and my cards have all arrived on time. That must be a record.'

Isa nodded. 'When I was your age, I hated to get my cards when it was all over. Somehow it's never the same! Nowadays, of course, I'm glad when people forget my birthday,' she added with a chuckle. 'Anyway, we must have a wee celebration tea tonight. Do you like chocolate cake? People say Morag makes a very nice one.'

'Oh, you mustn't bother,' Beverley said quickly. 'I didn't mean to tell you, but when I saw the cards, well——'

It was Isa's curiosity that had caused her to mention it, but she didn't like to say this.

'You're not going out to Solan this morning, are you?' Isa asked.

'No, I have the morning off,' Beverley replied. 'I've some things to buy, and I've arranged to have my hair done.'

'It would be nice if Alex would give you the afternoon

too, seeing it's your birthday. I'll ask him if you like,' said Isa.

Beverley sat up with a jerk. 'You mustn't tell him it's my birthday,' she said quickly. 'I don't want him to think I'm looking for any favours. Goodness knows, he hasn't a very high opinion of me—not since I lost the boat.'

But later on, Beverley found—as she had guessed—that Isa had not kept the news to herself.

When she went down to breakfast, Morag gave her a quick smile and said, 'Happy birthday, Beverley,' while Isa caught her eye, glanced towards Alex, and shook her head. So Isa had asked him—only to be refused! Beverley thought with annoyance. How she wished Isa had not done it!

Apart from a gruff 'good morning', Alex seemed absorbed in taking his porridge, and occasionally glancing at a letter beside his plate. But then it was always like this with him, thought Beverley bitterly. The envelope that held the letter bore a foreign stamp. Probably some stuffy old professor enquiring how many guillemots there were on Solan! Just the sort of thing that would hold Alex's full attention!

After a while he looked up briefly. 'By the way, Beverley, if you're going to the village this morning, I wonder if you'd ask Donald MacKenzie to let me have that sheet of tarpaulin he promised me. Tell him tomorrow will be soon enough.'

And, without waiting for her reply, he pushed the letter into the envelope, thrust it into his jacket pocket, got to his feet, and with a muttered word of excuse strode from the room.

Beverley finished her breakfast seething with resentment. He might have had the politeness to wish her a happy birthday, even if he hadn't the decency to give her the day off by way of celebration!

But as she walked towards the village she began to

simmer down. It was impossible on such a wonderful day to harbour resentment for long. The sun shimmered on the water and wildflowers bordered the road. The breeze that blew from the machair was scented, and larks soared in the cloudless blue sky, trilling their exquisite song.

First she headed for MacKenzie's general shop near the pier. She must send postcards to her family, she decided, and was delighted to find a coloured photograph of Kinneil Guesthouse showing the garden in full bloom. She picked one of these for her mother and wrote, 'The top left-hand window is mine. I can see Solan from it, first thing in the morning.' For her father and brother she chose stern views of the rocky cliffs. After reminding Donald MacKenzie about the tarpaulin she turned down the village street to the little house with 'Alison MacLean, Hairdresser', in a neat plaque on the white-painted gatepost.

The village hairdresser must rarely tend hair more lovely than her own, thought Beverley, for Alison had a wonderful mane of luxuriant waves and curls, the colour of a polished chestnut. In the dimness of her little cottage her hair gleamed and shimmered. Her husband was in the Navy and they had twin boys with hair even brighter than their mother's.

'I'm all in a flutter this morning,' she admitted to Beverley as she ran hot water, and tested the temperature of the spray with her hand. 'Lynne Redfern is arriving today and, would you believe it, she rang me from Fort William to make an appointment. It's important to please her because it might mean I should have some of her smart friends around the tenth of the month, when they arrive for her birthday party.'

'What's she like—really, I mean?' Beverley asked. 'I've heard so much about her, but somehow I can't picture her.'

'Well, she has lovely hair,' Alison told her as she tucked a towel about Beverley's shoulders. 'Fair, you understand,

and natural too! She doesn't use any bleach. She likes to leave it to the sun of the Hebrides to do the trick, and I must say she's right.'

Alison was busy trimming Beverley's dark hair when the door opened, and in came a girl whom Beverley did not have to be told was Lynne Redfern.

She was tall—rather too tall perhaps, Beverley decided. But she was so slim and carried her clothes with such flair that, in her case, it didn't seem to matter. She wore a cream silk dress with a crimson scarf tucked into the neckline and over her shining fair hair, which hung below her shoulders, was a floppy-brimmed hat of leaf-brown.

'Don't worry about me, Alison,' said Lynne, as Alison began to apologise for still being engaged on Beverley's hair. 'The ferry was early today. I think I'm a bit before time.'

She sank into a chair, took up one of the rather dog-eared magazines and flipped carelessly through the pages. For a moment her eyes met Beverley's in the mirror and Beverley saw that the newcomer's were of a strange vivid green. Altogether a disturbing person, this Lynne Redfern. No wonder she had made her mark with Alex! There was something vital and striking about her that demanded attention.

Alison seemed to feel it too, because she hurried over Beverley's hair and, when she was under the dryer, immediately began to attend to Lynne.

The sound of the dryer prevented Beverley from hearing what they were saying. But they seemed on very friendly terms and it was clear that the hairdresser was giving Lynne the gen on all that had happened on Kinneil since her last visit.

She herself was included in this, Beverley realised, as she saw Lynne swing around and give her an acute glance with eyes that were none too friendly. What had Alison been saying about her? Beverley wondered. She didn't appear to be a malicious girl, yet there could be no doubt about Lynne's sharp unfriendly look.

She was soon to learn when, at last, she was released from the dryer, while Lynne, her hair now shampooed, sat with a towel about her shoulders.

CHAPTER FIVE

'I FEEL I know you,' began Lynne, 'almost as if we'd been introduced! Alison tells me you're Beverley Nesbitt and that you're assisting Alex Ramage on Solan Island.'

When Beverley agreed that this was true, Lynne went on, 'I must say I don't envy you the job. You see, I'm Lynne Redfern and for a while I helped Alex, and it really was disastrous. I happened to break a jar containing one of those ghastly specimens of his, and he was furious. He's quite a grizzly bear, isn't he? I can't imagine why I like him so much! But then he probably approves of *you*. You'll have some scientific training, I suppose?' she added casually.

Just a little too casually, Beverley thought.

There was a pause as Lynne waited for a reply and Beverley could have kicked herself for feeling so ashamed of the fact that, far from being a scientist, her business was to take care of the black house. She was aware too of Alison listening attentively to their conversation.

'No, I'm not trained,' she told Lynne quietly.

'No?' The girl raised her eyebrows and looked faintly puzzled. 'Then what on earth *do* you do?' She gave a little laugh without amusement. 'There must be more to this than meets the eye. You're not being modest, are you, and hiding some sort of particular talent?'

Beverley swallowed, reluctant to admit that she was no more than Alex's dogsbody. 'I—I sort of help with the domestic side of the work,' she said at last.

'Oh!' A certain subtle change took place in the other girl's attitude. 'What you mean is that you sort of house-keep for him at the black house, is that it?'

'Sort of!' Beverley admitted.

'But how do you stand it?' Lynne asked sympathetically. 'The black house is too ghastly for words.'

'Oh, we've fixed it up quite a lot,' Beverley assured her. 'It's quite nice now.'

'Is it indeed! I can't imagine anyone being able to make anything of it. However, as long as you're satisfied, that's the main thing, isn't it? By the way,' she changed the subject as she swung around towards a mirror as Alison began to comb and set her hair, 'my birthday's on the tenth, and I'm having a party as usual this year. And just in case we don't meet again beforehand, I'd like to invite you now.'

'Thank you, but——' Beverley began.

But Lynne broke in. 'No, don't say no! You must come. We're all one big happy family here on Kinneil and we don't stand on ceremony.'

'I should love it,' Beverley found herself saying calmly, then immediately felt dismayed. It was obvious that the yearly party was a very big occasion on Kinneil, and she had brought nothing suitable with her to wear.

Soon it was Lynne's turn to have her hair dried, and Alison was able to unpin Beverley's hair and comb it into soft waves.

As Beverley was about to leave, Lynne popped her head out from under the dryer. 'See you at the Castle on the tenth,' she called. 'Alex will be there, and so will the MacCrimmons, I expect. They usually come. They're old dears really, although I get the impression they rather disapprove of me,' she added laughingly and, with a wave of her hand, ducked her head back under the dryer.

Yes, Lynne Redfern was pretty and sophisticated and her clothes were superbly cut, but there was a hardness in the green eyes and something veiled and antagonistic in her manner, Beverley decided, as she went along the village street.

And no wonder!

If, as Isa had said, Lynne had marked Alex Ramage down for her own, the thought that Beverley was sharing his life on Solan would be anything but welcome. Still Lynne was civilised enough to be polite, no matter how she felt, and Beverley fervently hoped things would remain like this, although she had the uncomfortable impression that Lynne was a girl of many moods and would make a bad enemy.

Isa was in the garden when Beverley got back to the guesthouse.

'It looks as if this is going to be a good year for roses,' Isa said with satisfaction, as she tied up the ramblers. 'I'm so glad you were able to stay on! You will see the garden at its best. Well, have you any news for me? Did you see anyone interesting on your travels?'

'I met Miss Redfern. She was in Alison's getting her hair done, and she invited me to her birthday party.'

'Now that *is* nice!' Isa said with satisfaction. 'You know, it's strange about the Redferns. The father and mother are so nice, and try their best to become part of things here on Kinneil, but somehow they never quite make it. They're always outsiders in spite of all their efforts. Lynne is really a very pretty girl. I can't imagine why she hasn't got a husband for herself by now, instead of setting her sights on Alex Ramage. I simply don't see him fitting into her way of life. He's not the sort of man to waste his time at smart parties and would be bored to death with society small-talk.'

'Of course, as far as the party on the tenth is concerned, I shan't be able to go,' Beverley told her. 'I haven't brought anything suitable. I didn't think my stay here would include such a grand affair. A local ceilidh was as far as my mind went, and I certainly don't intend to go to the expense of buying anything very special that's going to be worn only on one occasion. I'll simply have to ask Alex to let me have a holiday on that day. I could take the ferry to Skye. I'd like to see something of it while I'm here. I could spend the night there and come back in the morning, if there's a boat returning. I must see how I can arrange the times.'

'You musn't think of such a thing,' Isa protested. 'It wouldn't do at all if you didn't go to Lynne's party. We're great gossips here on Kinneil and people would remark on it. As to the dress, we must see what can be done about it,' she added a little mysteriously.

'Oh, well, I'd better be heading for Solan,' Beverley said with a sigh. 'It would have been nice to have had the day off, but evidently my lord and master has different views.'

'Alex Ramage can be very provoking at times,' Isa agreed. But Beverley was surprised to note that, instead of her usual air of disapproval when she spoke of him, Isa had a slight twinkle in her eye. 'It's beyond me what a great favourite he is among the girls, when he has such an offputting manner.'

'Well, here's one girl he's not a favourite with!' Beverley said pettishly, as she reluctantly left the bright garden and went indoors.

After lunch she changed into her working clothes of jeans and sweater and as it was ebb tide set off to walk across to Solan, pausing now and then to pick up some of the shells that to her were irresistible. Why had Alex refused to give her the day off? she was asking herself irritably, as she continued on her way. After all, everything had been made easy for him. Morag had cut sandwiches for him, and he had agreed readily enough to brew up a pot of tea at lunch time. After lunch there was rarely much that required seeing to at the black house, because she had now got it into good order.

When she arrived there was no sign of life about the black house and, irritably, she pushed open the door with more force than was necessary; then gave a little gasp, as she saw behind the armchair the shell screen glimmering in the rays of sunlight through the small window.

She moved across the floor and touched it gently. This was the very best birthday present she could have had. So this was why Alex had insisted on her coming to Solan that afternoon! He had had this lovely surprise in store for her!

'Well, do you like it?' Alex's deep voice spoke from the doorway.

She swung around, her face radiant with pleasure. 'I think it's simply beautiful! What a lovely surprise! You are a dear, Alex!'

Impulsively she got on tiptoe and aimed a kiss in the general direction of his cheek. But she had not allowed for his great height. Her kiss missed its mark and alighted in a haphazard sort of way on his chin.

And now suddenly she was left feeling foolish.

This was exactly the sort of impulsive action he would despise. 'Sorry!' she mumbled, and was on the point of turning away when she felt herself caught up by two massive hands around her waist.

'What about giving me a proper one?' he said quietly.

His eyes were hazel, she realised, with dark golden flecks, the colours one sees in a swiftly running burn, shot through by the rays of the sun. Selfconsciously she gave him a pecking kiss on the cheek.

'Is that the best you can do?' he asked dryly. 'It seems to me, Beverley , that you haven't the courage of your convictions.' Slowly he lowered her to the ground.

On her feet once more, she regained her composure. 'I don't know what you mean by that,' she told him.

'Don't you? What I mean is that if you intended to kiss me, why did you chicken out at the last moment? Why not make a proper job of it?'

'But I didn't really intend to! I did it on the spur of the

moment. You see, I was so pleased and excited to see the shell screen,' she added hastily.

'Really? You disappoint me,' he replied. 'For a moment I thought there was a little more to it than that!'

'Really, Alex Ramage, you are the most conceited man!' she flared. 'Do you really think I go around kissing men indiscriminately?'

'I hadn't really thought about it,' he said solemnly. 'But now you mention it, I'll give it my full consideration.'

His hazel eyes twinkled down at her and suddenly she burst into laughter.

'That's better!' he observed. 'And now what about declaring a truce—at least for your birthday?'

She was immediately wary. 'You mean that after today you'll go back to being your usual unbearable self?'

'Is that any way to speak to your boss?'

And again she felt laughter bubbling up.

'Come, Beverley, I'm not such a dragon as you think! Let's spend the afternoon exploring Solan. You have never seen it properly, you know! Make up a flask of tea and cut some sandwiches!'

The order was given in his usual dictatorial way, and as she obeyed Beverley had to smile, because it was plain that he intended to treat her nicely, yet couldn't resist being bossy; it was just his nature.

'You would make some woman a very overbearing husband,' she told him, as she cut bread and buttered it. Then, placing thick slices of ham on the bread, she made sandwiches just as she knew he liked them. She added some scones she had made on the previous day, a flask of tea, and some fruit, and placed them all in a wicker basket.

Alex took the binoculars from behind the door and flung them about his shoulders. 'Yes, I suppose you're right. I should make some unfortunate woman a very undesirable husband, I'm afraid. But marriage is something I'm not going to think about, until this project on Solan is completed. And I'm going to tell you why this very afternoon.'

'Oh!' was all she found to say to this unexpected remark.

They went out and across the island, over the machair, where their feet sank deep in wild flowers. A soft breeze ruffled Beverley's hair, and although Alex had relapsed into silence she could feel a strange warmth and comfort in the presence of this tall man who strode beside her.

The machair gave way to sand-dunes as they went into one of the little bays, where they found a sheltered spot with their backs to a great boulder. Sheltered from the breeze, Beverley took the things out of the basket, and they ate in companionable silence, their eyes on the sea, the water stranded with green and blue, and shading into a deep purple blue that was almost violet.

Alex's first words were unexpected. 'I like your new hairstyle.'

'What? So you noticed?' she laughed, surprised and pleased.

'Yes, I noticed. In fact, I notice quite a lot, but that doesn't mean I talk about everything I'm aware of. For instance, I get the impression sometimes that you're rather impatient with the work I do. You don't seem to feel that it's really important.'

'Oh!' Beverley felt quite taken aback. So he was aware of her occasional moments of annoyance!

'You've told me you hated working in an office,' he continued. 'Well, perhaps you'll be interested to know that I can sympathise, because I've experienced something of the same kind.'

She looked at him in surprise. 'You mean that at one time you worked in an office?'

'Not quite. You see, I was born on a croft in Islay.'

Islay! The island of the Lords of the Isles, Beverley was thinking. So she had not been so far out when, in her own mind, she had associated him with the hero, Somerled, who had ruled from that beautiful island.

'Yes, on a croft,' he continued. 'It's true no one can become rich owning a croft, but at the same time there are many compensations. There's the feeling of being your own boss—that all the responsibilities are on your own shoulders. The life is varied and, above all, it's an outdoor life. And even as a boy I knew that this was what I wanted above everything else. But my parents felt differently. They wanted to see me educated, so I was sent to an uncle in London. It was from his home that I went to school. I needn't tell you how much I hated living in a city. But as I grew older I found some compensation in long country walks at the weekends. I quickly discovered that it was the animals and plants that really interested me. I've studied in the English countryside and in Wales, but I've always known that what I want is to get back to Scotland— permanently, that is! So you can imagine how important this project on Solan is to me. I'm determined to make a success of it, and I shall struggle not to have to leave Scotland again.'

Beverley bit her lip, feeling ashamed of herself. She had been so impatient at times! But now she would know better.

'Well, so much for that!' said Alex, getting to his feet. 'But I thought things might go smoother between us, if we had a talk and tried to straighten things out. And now I want to show you where I shall be working for the next few weeks.'

They went northwards this time, the land mounting to a great cliff that fell hundreds of feet into a sea that boiled and smashed against the base.

He took her to one side of this where she could get a good view along the surface of the cliff. She could see hundreds of birds nestling on narrow ledges on the bare rock.

'Look!' He handed her the binoculars. 'Do you see that great bird? That's a solan goose. It's from it that the island gets its name. Part of my job will be to ring some of these birds.'

As Beverley watched she saw a bird plunge into the sea with great white wings, tipped with black. 'Why, it's enormous!' she exclaimed.

'Yes. They have wings six feet in span. They're one of the largest of all seabirds. We must make another expedition here later on, when you'll be able to see the young; they look just like big powder-puffs.'

And now she moved the glasses to the top of the cliff, and as she did so, burst out laughing. 'What are those birds with the great funny beaks?'

'Those are puffins,' he told her. 'They're the clowns of the bird world.'

Beverley was laughing as she watched their antics. They strutted about on the cliff top looking so very pompous and solemn. Their backs were black, the front white: they had great broad bills coloured bright red and yellow with grey circles ringing the cheeks and eyes.

'Oh yes, the puffin always looks as if he were about very important business,' Alex told her. 'But they don't stay long on Solan. They arrive in early summer, and are gone by the end of August.'

There were many birds of different varieties on the cliffs and Beverley listened entranced as Alex named them for her and described their habits. It was a scene of wild beauty: the sea beating wildly against the cliffs, the great varieties of bird life and, on top of the cliff, a great spread of wild hyacinth like a glowing sea of violet-blue flowing back towards the interior of the island.

At last, reluctantly, she handed him back the glasses and slowly they made their way back across the island to the black house.

As they returned to Kinneil she cautiously questioned him about the yearly party at Kinneil Castle. 'I expect everyone dresses up to the nines,' she said, and waited eagerly for his reply.

He nodded. 'Yes, it's one time in the year when we really go the whole hog. Most of the men wear full Highland evening dress—kilt, lace jabot, silver buckles, the lot! And the women put on their best finery. But in spite of all the grandeur we enjoy ourselves thoroughly. Anyway, it's the kind of old place that seems to suit that sort of thing. But why the interest in Kinneil Castle?'

For a moment Beverley hesitated. Somehow she felt a little shy about telling him of her problem. Then, with a rush, she said, 'I met Lynne Redfern at Alison's today when I was getting my hair done, and she invited me to the party. But it's really a ball, isn't it? And I didn't bring anything suitable with me. I thought life would be pretty rough and ready in these parts. At the most I thought my social life wouldn't involve anything more than a ceilidh.'

'Life here is pretty rough and ready most of the time, but we do have our moments of grandeur. But why worry about clothes? As long as you enjoy yourself, does it matter what you wear? Although I would draw the line at your present get-up,' he remarked, as he surveyed her work-worn jeans and sweater.

Beverley sighed with exasperation. How typical of the man to dismiss her problems so lightly! 'It's all very well for you! You'll be looking terrific in your Highland finery,' she told him.

'Thanks!' And she saw with annoyance that he was actually grinning. 'Somehow I was always under the impression that I was an ugly sort of chap. You've quite restored my self-confidence.'

'Your self-confidence doesn't need the slightest boosting,' she told him crossly.

With a laugh he turned the boat and headed it towards the tiny pier on Kinneil.

When they arrived at the guesthouse, they were met by Isa. Her manner was mysterious and Beverley noticed that, as she crossed the hall, Isa closed the parlour door, as though she didn't want her to see inside.

But Beverley dismissed Isa's unusual manner from her mind as she went upstairs to wash and change.

Later, when she went downstairs again she discovered

what all the mystery was about, for the parlour had been transformed. A fire of beech logs glowed in the wide chimney and pulled up near it was an old oak table crammed with goodies of every kind and brightened by a candelabrum holding three crimson candles. The silver shone, and the crystal sparkled. Bowls of flowers ornamented nearly every piece of available furniture. On a silver salver on a side table was a birthday cake elaborately ornamented with pink and white icing on which 'Happy Birthday, Beverley' had been written in white icing.

As she stammeringly expressed her thanks the sisters smiled delightedly 'We thought we should mark the occasion, seeing you're away from home for your birthday,' Morag told her.

'Yes,' Isa put in, 'and this is from both of us.'

And as Beverley pulled open the ribboned package Isa handed to her, she gave a little gasp of pleasure, for it contained the exquisite piece of Thai silk which she had so admired.

'We want you to have it made into a gown for the party at Kinneil Castle,' Isa told her. 'Morag will make it for you. All you have to do is to show her what style you want. After tea we'll clear the table and you can pick out something from a pattern-book I got from Alison. She takes a great interest in fashion, so you'll probably see something you fancy.'

'But I couldn't,' Beverley demurred. 'It's so beautiful. Couldn't one of you use it yourself?'

'Now you mustn't refuse,' said Morag, evidently prepared for opposition. 'Neither Isa nor myself are young enough to look well in anything so elaborate. You must wear it at Lynne's party and do us credit by looking simply stunning.'

Isa nodded. 'Yes, it will make a wonderful dress for the occasion. You know, Beverley, we're beginning to look upon you as a member of the family. Let's not argue about it any more. The food will be getting cold.'

As the sisters whisked into the kitchen, Alex came into the room. 'What's going on here?' he asked in amazement.

'It's for my birthday,' Beverley said a little shyly. 'Isa and Morag are giving me a party.'

He raised his eyebrows in mock affront. 'Are they indeed! Well, it's more than they ever did for me!' He surveyed the laden table, the candles and the birthday cake with its inscription with growing surprise. 'It seems to me, Beverley, that you've scored a hit with the MacCrimmons.'

'You sound surprised,' she told him tartly. 'And I can't say I'm altogether flattered.'

'I didn't intend to flatter you,' he replied bluntly.

Beverley smiled impishly. 'Do you know, I think you're jealous, because the MacCrimmons gave no party for your birthday. Hasn't it occurred to you that, from the way you behave, people imagine you're too high and mighty to enjoy simple things, like a party?'

'Me, high and mighty?' His voice rose incredulously. 'Whatever gave you that idea?'

Beverley laughed outright. 'Oh, I don't know! Just a passing thought!'

He frowned at her with that lowering of the eyebrows that Beverley had secretly begun to call 'Alex's glower.' Before he could say anything more Isa and Morag returned bearing steaming platters of food.

As usual with the MacCrimmons' Scottish hospitality, Beverley found it a little overwhelming. It was difficult to refuse as the sisters pressed one plate after another on her, tutting and remarking that she wasn't eating a bite.

It was one of the happiest birthdays she could remember; and she was surprised to see how Alex joined in the lighthearted chatter, evidently determined to make the occasion as pleasant and happy as possible.

When it came time to blow out the candles and cut her birthday cake it was Alex who carried it over to the table and, with his large brown hand, helped her to cut through the thick royal icing.

'Goodness, but you do look like bride and groom!' Isa exclaimed. And Beverley saw Morag dart her a warning glance.

'I'm afraid you're far from the mark,' Alex remarked easily. 'From what I gather Beverley is a dedicated career girl.'

But in spite of his pleasant way of speaking, Beverley got the impression that he resented Isa's remark and for a moment she felt the return of the old animosity towards him.

She forgot her resentment as the meal came to an end and they all joined together in carrying the dishes out to the kitchen. Isa took the candelabrum from the table and when the cloth had been removed, took down a fat book of fashion plates.

'There's no doubt about it, Alison has a great gift for fashion,' Isa said as she opened the book wide and drew up chairs. 'There are not many women on the island who take the same interest that she does, so I imagine anything you pick out of this will be pretty up to date and on the ball, as they say.'

The three women sat around the table, turning over the leaves of the illustrated fashion book, while Alex drew up an armchair to the fire, flung on an extra log, then, leaning back, filled his pipe from a jar on the small table beside his chair. And, as they began discussing the different styles, Beverley stole a glance at him and saw that he was gazing into the fire, his mind evidently miles away.

It was soon clear that each of the sisters had her own idea of what would be best for Beverley. Isa was all in favour of an elaborate tiered skirt, while Morag favoured the exact opposite. When they had finished arguing, Beverley felt completely confused.

'I think the only thing to do is to ask Alex to decide,' Morag said.

Isa and Beverley looked at her in surprise, as they envisaged his abrupt refusal.

But at that moment Alex who, after all, must have been listening to their conversation, got to his feet and coming to the table looked over Beverley's shoulder and solemnly studied the pages as Isa turned them.

'I'm all for the one with the flounces,' Isa told him, 'but Morag prefers this one, although, in my opinion, it's much too severe.'

'How about you?' he asked, glancing down at Beverley.

Beverley shook her head. 'I'm completely at sea. I simply can't make up my mind.'

'Very well,' he said. 'Keep turning, and I'll tell you when to stop.'

For a few moments there was silence in the cosy parlour, then he said, 'Now that's my choice!' tapping with his pipe stem a simple pattern with smooth flowing lines. 'It suits the material, and what's more, it will suit Beverley.'

As the two sisters regarded the illustration doubtfully, he turned to Beverley. 'Well, what do you think of it?'

She nodded slowly. 'Yes, I think it strikes just the right note. Not too fussy, yet not too formal.'

'Exactly!' he agreed with finality.

This was his usual brusque, decisive manner, and the three women burst into laughter.

He looked faintly surprised. 'Have I said anything amusing?'

'No, just that you sound more like your usual bossy self,' Beverley said teasingly. But she was pleased at the interest he was taking. It was obvious that he expected her to do him credit on the big night and the thought warmed her heart.

And as the days sped by she found herself looking forward more and more eagerly to the night of the ball when she would arrive at Kinneil Castle in her wonderful new dress, and escorted by Alex Ramage.

CHAPTER SIX

To Beverley's delight, Isa's estimation of her sister's skill as a dressmaker quickly proved to be correct, for the dress, as it progressed, turned out to have the touch of the professional. And the amazing thing was that Morag managed to do it all on an old-fashioned hand sewing-machine which she kept under a wooden cover on a windowsill in the kitchen.

In the evenings, when Beverley returned to Kinneil it was to find Morag busily turning the handle of the sewing-machine, while Isa finished the preparation of the evening meal.

'You could easily take your place in the world of haute couture,' Beverley told her.

Morag looked up and laughed dryly. 'I'm afraid I shouldn't know my way around in that world! I'd be quite lost! But I do think this is going to look pretty presentable.'

When she discovered how wonderfully the dress was turning out, Beverley found herself looking forward more than ever to Lynne's birthday party. Thinking about it, she absentmindedly burnt a panful of chops while cooking lunch at the black house. Guiltily she dumped them under a clump of bracken and decided to start all over again, for Alex was nearly always late for meals, and nothing she could say made the smallest difference.

But, as ill-luck would have it, on this particular occasion he happened to be on time. She had barely set another panful sizzling when the door swung open and he came in.

Across his broad shoulders was a rough sack from which came growling and spitting sounds. He carried it carefully into that part of the black house where in olden days cattle had been sheltered in winter. Beverley deserted her post at the stove and followed, curious as the sounds became louder and the heaving of the sack more furious as he cautiously unfastened the rough twine that fastened the top.

Inside were two of the most enchanting kittens she had ever seen. 'Oh, what little darlings!' she exclaimed. 'Where did you find them?'

'I found these "little darlings", as you call them, in a ditch. They must have been abandoned by their mother and they're not old enough to fend for themselves.'

But she was hardly listening. Impulsively she had put out her hand to stroke the thick fur.

'Be careful!' he exclaimed.

But it was too late. Those charming furry faces had become transformed by snarling rage. Spitting and hissing, they lashed out with razor-sharp claws. Beverley gave a scream and drew back, blood dripping from her lacerated hand.

Alex gave a grunt of annoyance. 'Don't you realise that these are not ordinary kittens? They are the kits of a wild-cat.'

Quickly he retied the sack and fetched bandages and lotion from the first-aid box on top of the dresser.

'But they look so much like tabbies,' she protested a little shakily, as he bandaged her hand with swift deft movements that seemed surprising in such a big man.

'They may seem so to you, but not to anyone who knows anything about wildcats. I'll have a splendid opportunity to study them here. They certainly were a lucky find.'

'What!' she cried. 'You don't really mean you're going to keep them here?'

'Why not?' he demanded. 'Now you've had a taste of what they're like, you'll be more careful in future—especially as they grow bigger. Anyway, I don't intend to keep them indefinitely. As soon as they're able to fend for themselves, I'll return them to the wild.'

Beverley looked at him doubtfully. 'And in the mean-while you're going to keep them here in the black house?'

'And why not?' He seemed surprised at her question. 'They'll be perfectly all right.'

'It's not *them* I'm thinking of,' Beverley said tartly. 'They seem so savage. But perhaps they'll grow tamer in time,' she added hopefully. Now that she had got over her first shock, and her hand was comfortably bandaged, she made an effort to adjust to this new situation.

'I'm afraid you're being optimistic,' he told her. 'It's never been known for true wildcats to be tamed, no matter how young they're caught.'

But Beverley was no longer listening. Clouds of blue smoke were rising from the cooker. With an exclamation of dismay she raced to the other end of the room and snatched the pan from the flaring burner. 'Oh, not again!' she wailed.

'Don't let's bother about lunch today,' Alex put in. 'Make a sandwich or something for yourself. I'll be too busy with these two little monsters to bother about eating at the moment. The first thing I must do is find a coop and put them safely out of harm's way.'

He disappeared into an outbuilding while Beverley ruefully disposed of the smoking pan. In a few minutes he returned with a big wooden packing case.

He ripped off the top and nailed wire-netting across it. Then putting on strong gloves he edged the kits inside one at a time. As he did so they spat and snarled, their tiny teeth digging ferociously into the gloves. And Beverley noticed with alarm how savagely they crawled upside-down on the netting, once they were inside, in an attempt to escape and get at their captor.

'I do hope they're safe enough there,' she said doubt-fully.

Alex leaned back against the table with a sigh of relief. 'Well, that's done, thank goodness! They're hardly strong enough yet to force the netting, but give them a few weeks and there'll be hardly any box they won't be able to get out of.'

'Well, at least that'll be something to look forward to!' Beverley retorted tartly.

But Alex was in such good humour at his find that he ignored her remark. 'Yes, the genuine article!' he congratulated himself, regarding the two writhing furry little animals with satisfaction. 'Do you see the flat ears and the black tips to the tails and the way the stripes form the letter "M" on the foreheads? All typical signs of the genuine article.'

Then, to her annoyance, apparently forgetting that he had decided not to have a meal, he rubbed his hands together and said cheerfully, 'Well, let me have something to eat now! I must get across to Kinneil and fetch feed for them. Ordinary cat-food should do nicely, and plenty of milk, of course!'

Exasperatedly Beverley watched from the door as his receding figure strode through the bracken towards the shore. There was a buoyancy in his step and a boyishness in his manner that she had not noticed before. What an extraordinary mixture he was, she thought. As far as she was concerned, he was a complete enigma. But as she began to clean up the greasy stove she had to admit to herself that when he wasn't there the black house seemed empty and deserted.

The arrival of the kits made a vast difference to Beverley's way of life. Her routine had to be adapted to Alex's obsessive interest in the kits. Instead of setting off in the mornings for the cliffs on the north side of the island to study bird life, he spent most of his day at the black house, observing and noting the ways of the kits. Soon he began to spend his time at the table absorbed in textbooks or writing steadily for hours at a time. His temper, she noted a little wryly, had improved a great deal since their arrival. But he did not believe in wasting his time in idle chit-chat and often she would sigh in exasperation as she moved about quietly doing the daily chores, feeling more like the ghost of some former tenant of the black house than like a living human being. Sometimes she was tempted to bang something very sharply in the hope of waking him up to her presence, but she decided against it, feeling sure that such marks of independence would be greeted with a glare.

She was surprised to find that after a while she too was being caught up in the fascination of the new arrivals. They were always so full of interest. They were a male and female, and soon Beverley was engaged in trying to think of names for them. Alex too took an unexpected interest in thinking of something suitable. As they sat at lunch they would vie with each other, amidst shouts of laughter, to think of something appropriate.

'How about Sammy and Samantha?' suggested Beverley. 'Or Romeo and Juliet?'

This made Alex laugh so hard that she was forced to abandon it.

'A bit too romantic for those two young devils, isn't it? Though, come to think of it, they'd both be pretty good at climbing balconies. No, I'm afraid we'll have to think of something more prosaic. How about Punch and Judy?'

Beverley wrinkled her nose. 'Not very inspired! But I suppose it is more suitable.'

'No, I suppose it's not romantic enough for you.'

She was aware that Alex was watching her closely and was aware that her cheeks had turned pink, as she said airily, gathering up the plates, 'What makes you think I'm romantic?'

'You forget my job makes me observant,' he told her dryly. 'In fact there are quite a few of your traits that haven't escaped my notice.'

Hurriedly Beverley began to wash the dishes. It was on the tip of her tongue to ask exactly what he had noticed, but she decided she wouldn't give him the satisfaction of knowing she cared.

As the days passed she became increasingly irritated by his long silences as he sat writing, occasionally glancing through the open door as though in search of inspiration, and completely oblivious of her presence. But what she found hardest to endure was the cavalier way he treated the meals she so painstakingly prepared. He had an exasperating way of pulling up a chair to the table and then completely ignoring the plate she would place beside him while he turned over the leaves of his notebook with a muttered, 'Just leave it there! I'll have it later.'

Then one day all her suppressed resentment seemed to boil over in a sudden burst of fury. It was triggered off by the fact that she had prepared what she considered a particularly tasty meal. It had been cold by the time Alex finally tackled it. When he finished she swept the dishes up in grim silence and said as quietly as she could, although her voice trembled with rage, 'If you've nothing more for me to do, I'd like to go across to Kinneil. Perhaps I could get my hair done—that's if you've no objection,' she added sarcastically.

He looked up and gave an absentminded wave of the hand. 'Of course not! Trot along! You must be bored here, there's so little for you to do.'

This was the last straw! Feeling that if she waited another moment she would throw something at him, Beverley seized her coat and darted out of the house, slamming the door behind her.

Rage consumed her as she trekked across the sand which had been uncovered at low tide. But by the time she had had her hair done at Alison's and had a gossip, she began to simmer down. Perhaps she might have a meal at the seafood restaurant near the pier, she decided, before returning to Solan.

But as she walked up to the small tables outside the restaurant she saw Lynne Redfern engrossed in conversation with a rather plump, elderly man. With her usual unerring eye for style Lynne was dressed in a featherweight tweed of a misty shade of blue. Even the little white West Highland terrier on a tartan lead that sat at her feet seemed to complete the picture of sophistication she presented.

When Lynne caught sight of her, she waved. 'Hello there! Come over, Beverley, and let me introduce George Clayton. He's a sort of cousin, way far out.'

George's small, rather piggy eyes surveyed Beverley closely. 'You must be the girl who's working for Alex Ramage. He has quite a name amongst us naturalists, you know.'

'Don't be ridiculous!' Lynne interjected contemptuously. 'You don't call yourself a naturalist just because you run a piddling little kids' zoo, or think you're in the same category as Alex.'

'You seem to forget,' George protested, 'that when I was left Meadowlands I hadn't a penny to keep it going. I had to start something, and I think a kid's zoo was a great idea. I've put a lot of work into it, and it's beginning to pay off. I only wish I had a few novelties. If only I could add something a bit unusual!'

'Alex certainly has something a bit unusual,' Beverley said bitterly, as she pulled up a chair, 'he's completely engrossed in the wildcat world now. That's why I'm over here, actually. I couldn't take any more of it. I thought I'd scream if I didn't get away for a while.'

'You mean to say,' George's eyes gleamed with interest, 'that Alex has actually caught a wildcat? I thought the last one had disappeared from this part of the world ages ago.'

'Not one, but two,' she told him. 'They're not fully grown, but they're getting bigger every day—and wilder too, for that matter.'

'But this is absolutely terrific!' George enthused. 'This is the very thing that would interest the kids at Meadowlands!'

'You mean to say you're going to add wildcats to the rides on dear little donkeys, and the pretty little ducks!' Lynne mocked.

'Why not?' George demanded a little belligerently. 'It's all very well for you to look down your nose, Lynne. You're loaded. You've nothing to worry about, but when I inherited Meadowlands I inherited nothing but a heap of debts. I have to make a living somehow.'

'But Meadowlands is a grotty little zoo for kids,' Lynne told him.

'With a couple of wildcats it wouldn't be so grotty,' George said mildly. 'I simply must see them,' he went on, turning to Beverley.

At his words Beverley felt a stab of alarm. She could visualise all too clearly what Alex's reaction would be if George turned up all eagerness to acquire one of his precious kits.

Her feelings must have shown all too clearly in her face, for Lynne said a little maliciously, 'You poor darling! I suppose Alex is being his usual insufferable self! No one knows better than I how high-handed he can be at times.'

George looked from one to the other. 'What's all this about?' he enquired.

'Just, dear George, that I don't feel you'll be particularly welcome.'

George looked bewildered. 'But why not? There's no reason why I shouldn't see the wildcats. And who knows, he might be glad enough to get rid of one of them.'

'No, no, you mustn't try to see them,' Beverley told him hurriedly. 'Alex is writing a paper on the kits and——' She stopped, feeling that this remark was a further indiscretion.

'But what's all the secrecy about?' George demanded. 'Why should he keep them to himself?'

'He simply doesn't want to be disturbed until he's finished his paper,' Beverley said desperately.

'Oh, I see—a real dog-in-the-manger! Well, if I were you

I shouldn't take any notice of him,' George told her earnestly. 'I've heard about this Alex Ramage. He's considered a very arrogant fellow, for all his so-called cleverness!'

'Yes, you mustn't be so protective of Alex, Beverley darling!' Lynne smiled with a hint of malice in her eyes. 'We'll pop over tomorrow at low tide and just beg a peep at the kits. They sound so amusing and interesting. I've never seen wildcats, and it would make a talking point.'

'I do wish you wouldn't,' Beverley urged. 'He'll be frightfully annoyed.'

'Don't tell me you're *frightened* of him!' cried Lynne. 'Really, Beverley, I should have thought you had more spirit. Well, he doesn't frighten *me*—not in the least. And George doesn't intend running away with the kits. Do you, George?'

George gave a chortling laugh. 'Not with two wildcats, I can assure you! But I don't see why I shouldn't have a look at them.'

'There, it's all arranged!' Lynne said with satisfaction. And as Beverley tried to put in a last desperate protest, she held up her hand. 'There's no use in trying to put George off! He has the hide of a rhinoceros, haven't you, George darling?'

George beamed as though he had been paid the most elaborate compliment. 'Well, I'll say this for myself, when I make up my mind, I usually get my way,' he said with satisfaction.

To Beverley's relief, a diversion was caused by the little dog, which jumped up on her lap and began to lick her hands with his small pink tongue. 'Oh, isn't he a darling!' Beverley exclaimed, stroking his thick white fur.

'Oh, he's a nice little thing!' Lynne agreed indifferently. 'But horribly spoiled. Actually he's a sort of pre-birthday present from Dad. I'd have preferred a Borzoi—they're so completely elegant. But the parents fell in love with

Mungo, and that was that.' She got to her feet. 'Come on, George, it's time you and I were heading home. I've a hundred and one things I want to do, and I expect you to make yourself handy.'

For a moment, words trembled on Beverley's lips, in the hope of dissuading them from the threatened visit, but with a little sigh she realised it would be no use. Under George's pompous manner she could detect a determination to get his own way. George had made up his mind to come to Solan and nothing she could say or do would put him off.

As Beverley fell asleep that night she was uneasily aware that the morning might prove singularly unpleasant. She had no doubt whatsoever that George and Lynne intended to pursue their plans, come what may, and it was with a feeling of profound relief that she awoke during the night to realise that one of those sudden storms that mark the Hebrides had blown up. She could hear the waves dashing against the shore and the wild howl of the wind as it buffeted her windowpanes. Probably, she thought hopefully, it would prove much too wild and discouraging for George and Lynne to set out for the island.

But when morning came she was disappointed to discover that the sky was a calm even blue, just as if the disturbance of the night had never existed. The weather in the Hebrides was certainly unpredictable, she thought sourly. She would have to accept that she was in for a distinctly unpleasant interview with Alex when he discovered the object of George's visit.

For once, Beverley had no objection when, as soon as they reached Solan, Alex settled down at the big table with his books and papers. He was his usual preoccupied self as he scribbled away and a peaceful silence reigned while Beverley busied herself with her usual chores, which now included scalding the dishes from which the kits ate. Alex had discovered early on that as Punch was more hefty than Judy he was inclined to gobble up her food as well as his own, and now they had to be carefully segregated at meal-times.

Occasionally she could not resist the temptation to sidle over to the window and watch anxiously as the tide receded and the sand became hard and golden. Now was the time when George and Lynne would be starting off from Kinneil.

Once, as she was staring anxiously into the distance, Alex's voice broke in, 'Why are you always standing at the window? You're not expecting anyone, are you?' He glanced at her suspiciously 'You haven't asked anyone over, have you? I mean, it would be an extraordinarily awkward time—just when I want to get this work finished.'

'Oh no, no, of course not!' she said hastily.

'Then you're terribly restless!' he told her irritably. 'Why can't you go for a walk if you can't settle down?'

'Oh, I was just going to prepare lunch,' she told him hastily. 'I thought of stew today,' she told him placatingly, knowing it was his favourite dish. 'I'll just pop out and get some water from the burn.'

She seized up a bucket and dashed out before he could question her further, for she had realised by now that very little escaped Alex's perspicacious glance. And she realised too that she was talking a little too quickly. He would be the first to notice the smallest change in her attitude towards him.

As she re-entered the black house she felt her heart sink, for Alex was standing by the window, binoculars glued to his eyes. He turned towards her. 'There are two people coming across the sands from Kinneil,' he announced abruptly. Then, before she had time to reply, he turned once more to the window and gazed steadily through the binoculars.

Beverley put down the bucket and began to assemble the meal with her back towards him, waiting tensely as she did so, knowing that before long he could be in no doubt as to who his visitors were.

'One of them is Lynne Redfern,' he told her. 'And the other is someone I've met before although I can't remember his name. But I know he's a short stout fellow who calls himself a naturalist, although as far as I can make out he's interested only in profit. He runs what he calls a sort of junior safari park, but he has no real interest in the scientific side of it. Now what on earth is making him come in this direction?'

He laid down the binoculars on the windowsill and thoughtfully paced the floor. 'I think I know what it is. He must have heard of the kits and he thinks he would have a terrific novelty if he could talk me into giving him one for his zoo. But how on earth did he hear about them?'

'You did buy lots of cat-food from MacKenzie's,' Beverley reminded him hastily. 'I mean, it was bound to get about. You know what a gossip MacKenzie is!'

'Um!' he said thoughtfully. 'Yes, MacKenzie is a great gossip. And, come to think of it, I remember that fellow's name. He's George Clayton. From all accounts, an incredible bore, and as tenacious as a mosquito. It's going to be difficult getting rid of him. And of course, knowing Lynne Redfern, I'm well aware she'll think it hilariously funny. Well, if George Clayton thinks he's going to waste my time he has another think coming. He'll find——'

He stopped suddenly, and fixing her with an eye that made her quail, said quietly but with a menace that quite startled her, 'It wasn't you, by any chance, was it?'

CHAPTER SEVEN

BEVERLEY hesitated in guilty silence and then said stammeringly, 'When I went over to Kinneil yesterday, I—I happened to meet Lynne and—George Clayton, and—and——'

'And of course you had to blab to them about my business, isn't that it?'

'Well, I did—did mention— the kits,' she quavered. 'I didn't—didn't think you'd mind. You see, George Clayton seemed so interested. And Lynne was asking me how I was getting along, and——'

'I can easily guess the rest,' he said bitterly. 'I suppose you poured into her ear what a miserable time you're having with me; how insufferable I am! And how, on top of everything else, you have a couple of wild kits to take care of! Was that it?'

This was so near the truth that Beverley could only swallow in silence.

'I can just see George Clayton's piggy little eyes gleaming with avarice when he heard about the kits,' said Alex. 'Do you realise how difficult it will be for me to get rid of that leech once he arrives, short of kicking him off the place! However, that's probably what I shall do,' he ended grimly.

By this time Beverley was reduced to such a state of misery that she almost welcomed the thought of George and Lynne's arrival. It would break up this horrible situation. 'But George said he only wanted to peep at them,' she protested weakly. 'After all, what harm can it do?'

'It can do this harm,' he replied. 'I'll be surprised if this

George Clayton can keep his mouth shut. Once he's seen the kits, he'll go about spreading the news and in no time I shall have hordes of trippers arriving at Solan "just to have a peep," as you call it. Well, as you've done the damage, you can pay the price!'

Seizing a piece of rope, he strode towards the boxes in which the kits were housed and quickly tied up each box. 'Take these up to the shieling in the woods and keep them there until this fellow goes. The boxes are awkward, but they're not too heavy for you to manage.' As he spoke he was thrusting the kits' feeding bowls, some tins of catfood and milk, together with tin openers and strong gauntlet gloves into a plastic bag. 'There, that's everything you'll need.'

'You don't mean me to take them—by myself?' Beverley protested feebly.

'Yes, who else?' he said tightly. 'Take them up to the woods—and hurry. I'll make short work of this Clayton fellow.'

'It was just that he was so very persistent,' she protested, as feeling as if she was in a dream she began to do as he insisted.

'He won't be so persistent when I'm finished with him,' Alex told her grimly.

As she was going through the door, carrying the boxes carefully, he flung at her the remark that stung her most. 'If I'd guessed what a gossip you were going to be, I shouldn't have taken you in the first place!'

By this time Beverley was so subdued that she sought in vain for words to defend herself.

As she disappeared into the woods she caught a glimpse of George and Lynne as they picked their way through the boulders that edged the shore of Solan at the point opposite Kinneil.

The kits were restless, spitting and hissing, and climbing wildly around inside their boxes so that Beverley had her work cut out to prevent the rope from being wrenched from her hand. It was a steep climb through the woods through clumps of bracken and trailing undergrowth until she reached the old abandoned shieling which at one time had been the hut used by shepherds grazing their flocks on Solan during the summer months. But now it was in ruins, the roof broken and sagging and the walls with gaping holes where the stones had fallen out. But it served sufficiently well as a shelter and she placed the boxes containing the kits in a dry corner. Then she went to the door.

From her eyrie she had a good view of Lynne and George Clayton advancing towards the black house. Even from the distance she could not mistake the grim air of unwelcome that permeated Alex's figure as he stood in the doorway. What line would he take with George? she wondered. And strangely enough she felt a sense of disappointment as after a few words the three figures moved into the black house. What had she expected? she wondered. A horrible scene, with George ejected from the island? Perhaps secretly she had thought this preferable to the churning jealousy she felt as she thought of Lynne acting as peacemaker between the two men. She was well aware that it had been Lynne's presence, her charm and beauty, that had persuaded Alex to invite them into the black house.

She seated herself on one of the fallen stones inside the hut, and waited, but eventually it was time for the kits to be fed. Beverley busied herself with opening the tins and arranging the food in the separate bowls.

Familiarity with the kits had made her careless and although she knew that Punch was wilder than Judy and stronger and every day growing more unmanageable she neglected to put on the second glove before she lifted him from his box. Perhaps it was the strangeness of the place that made him even wilder than usual, but as soon as she grasped him she knew she had made a great mistake. Suddenly he lashed out with those deadly sickle-shaped razor-sharp claws. In the nick of time she jerked back her hand and the claws missed their target. In the same instant he twisted free from her gloved right hand, leaped from the box and darted through one of the gaps in the wall. Unbelievingly Beverley gazed at the spot where he had vanished. Everything had happened with extraordinary rapidity and she simply could not take it in for a moment or two.

Then as the realisation flooded over her of how Alex would react when he discovered that one of his beloved kits had escaped, she ran towards the door. There had been a shower of rain which had passed away leaving the land bathed in fitful sunshine. But of the kit there was not the smallest sign. As she stood there looking at the landscape dotted with boulders and fern and copses of birch, rowan and alder and saw the thickness of the undergrowth she realised with a sense of doom that Punch was gone completely out of her reach. But she remained there for a while, her eyes anxiously searching the terrain in the vain hope that he might reappear.

What she did see was two figures leave the black house and make their way towards the shore. They were hurrying to get to Kinneil before the tide filled the channel between the two islands. No doubt, thought Beverley, in a very short time Alex would arrive at the shieling intent on carrying the kits back to the black house. How was she to admit to him that through carelessness she had allowed Punch to escape? The thought of the stormy scene ahead and the scathing remarks he would undoubtedly make galvanised her into action. After all, she thought, Punch had not had anything to eat. He was bound to be hungry and perhaps could be lured by a dish of food. There was also the fact that she had tried to teach the two kits their names. Was there just the possibility that he would come to her if she called him?

First she secured the wire netting over Judy's box. Then,

finding a stub of pencil and a crumpled piece of paper in her jacket pocket, she decided to scribble a note of explanation for Alex when he arrived. She bit on the pencil end as she cast around in her mind how best to word the message. Then, with a sigh of resignation, she realised there was no use beating about the bush. Better boldly to state the bald facts than to make ineffectual excuses which would only enrage him even more. She knew enough about Alex Ramage by this time to realise that to try to evade responsibility would be a very big mistake. 'Sorry,' she wrote, 'One of the kits has escaped. Am going in search of it.' Well, it was short and to the point, she thought wryly as she propped it up against the wall supported by a stone where he would see it as soon as he arrived.

As she went out she was met by a squall of rain carried almost horizontally by the wind which is so frequent in the Hebrides. She hadn't even taken her coat—not that any ordinary coat was of much use in such weather! One could be completely soaked in a few minutes. Luckily it was fairly mild and she decided to ignore the rain. There was nothing else to be done, except wait inside the shieling until Alex arrived and vented the full brunt of his fury upon her. No! Far better a lashing from the rain than from his merciless tongue when he realised that he had very probably lost Punch for good.

As she waded ankle-deep through the sodden and dripping bracken her shoes became heavy with water. Solan no longer seemed a paradise as a leaden mist hovered over the ground so that even the brilliantly coloured wildflowers were hidden by the floating veil. As she moved further and further away from the shieling Beverley was aware that the wretched Punch could be almost anywhere by this time. The small caverns between boulders, she knew, were favourite hiding places for wildcats, but there were thousands of these about the island and after several tries when she peered anxiously into the darkness and called Punch's name, only to receive silence, she was left with a feeling of complete hopelessness. Punch, it seemed, was lost for good. They would never see him again.

As her search lengthened and evening began to draw on, the rain, instead of lifting, grew heavier. Feeling cold, wet and completely miserable, she wandered into a little wood of birch and alder that formed a canopy above her head and cast a pale greenish glow that added to the eeriness of her surroundings. Unutterably exhausted, she sank down on to a lichen-covered log and, head in hands, tried to consider what she should do next. As she did so, it dawned on her that during her search for the kit she had back-tracked and wandered to such an extent that she was completely disorientated, and no longer had an idea of whereabouts in the island she now found herself. Although Solan was small enough it was a bewildering maze of woods and boulders so that different parts of it looked very similar.

She had no idea how long she remained there, but suddenly she sprang to her feet with a scream as an owl swept past her, its wings spectral in the gloomy light. Feeling exhausted, her weary mind began to fill with rather frightening thoughts. How was Alex going to react to the situation? Would he simply leave her to fend for herself as best she could? After all, to him Solan would appear ridiculously small. Since he knew every nook and cranny of his small domain would he think that she too ought to be able very easily to retrace her steps?

Apart from that, she knew only too well that he had an implacable streak. Her imagination conjured up a picture of him, his bony face set and unrelenting.

How long she sat there in utter wretchedness, she had no idea, but as darkness fell she was faced with the thought that Alex was making no attempt to find her. Was this then the nature of the man she had come to love? Alone in the darkness it seemed to come home to her that she was completely happy only in his presence. Her anger when he was absorbed in studying the kits had been due to the fact that at such times he was unaware of her. In the depths of her heart what she wanted was that she should be the sole object of his interest, yet to be love with Alex was to accept the man with all his quirks of character and his very detachment. These things contributed to the hold he had over her heart.

Then through the birch woods she saw a vague blurred light bobbing and weaving aimlessly. As she watched fascinated it seemed to vanish for a few moments and then to reappear even nearer. But it was definitely advancing towards her. And now a new terror struck her. There flashed into her mind stories she had heard from the MacCrimmon sisters as they sat by the peat fire in the evenings—stories of mysterious lights that had been seen in the Hebrides, lights that danced and swayed and invariably betokened death. She watched, horror-struck, as the bobbing light inexorably moved towards her. She sat petrified on the lichen-covered log, terrified to move a muscle.

Then she heard Alex's voice call her name. It sounded loud and to her ear held a note of anxiety. With a little cry of relief and happiness she jumped to her feet, power surging into her veins. With a little inarticulate exclamation she flung herself into his arms. 'I thought you'd never come,' she sobbed, her head close to the comforting roughness of his tweed jacket. For the moment she had completely forgotten the enmity that had arisen between them. All she knew was that, in his arms, she had found a haven. Her heart thudded with joy as his arms closed around her. If only this moment could last for ever, she thought, oblivious of the fact that rain was lashing down now with renewed vigour.

For a long moment Alex held her, his hand pressing her head close against his heart. Then gently and tenderly he smoothed her soaking hair. 'Poor darling, what a dreadful time you've had!'

Feeling a little lightheaded with relief, Beverley began

incoherently to explain how the kit had escaped.

He placed his finger on her lips. 'Not another word! There'll be plenty of time later for explanations.'

He picked up the lantern which he had placed on the ground and hung it on the branch of a tree. Then taking an oilskin cape from his pocket he wrapped it about her. In the light of the swaying lantern she could see his teeth flash briefly for a moment as he smiled. 'It's a bit like locking the stable door after the horse is gone, for you couldn't be much wetter than you are, but at least it will help to keep the wind out.'

'But—but what about the kit?' she stammered persistently. 'I know how important it is to you. We can't just leave it out here.'

'Not another word about the kit,' he commanded. 'This evening I realised how unimportant they are compared—— Oh well, I thought all sorts of things when Punch turned up at the black house on his own, and there was still no sign of you. It occurred to me that Solan would be pretty unendurable without you.'

Beverley felt her face grow pink with happiness and was glad that the darkness hid her reaction, and the surge of joy his words gave her. 'So Punch has come back!'

'Yes, young wildcats have a habit of returning to the place in which they're fed, you know. I found Punch waiting for me when I returned from Kinneil.'

'So you went to Kinneil?' she asked wonderingly.

'Yes, when Lynne and George Clayton tried to return they found that the tide had risen too high for them to cross back on foot. I was forced to take out the dinghy and take them home by boat, and of course the wretched thing chose to turn temperamental just as I was on the point of setting off again for Solan. I had to remain in Kinneil until it was fixed, so I had no idea you'd got yourself lost. In fact it didn't occur to me!'

'I'm afraid I've no bump of direction,' she told him ruefully.

'Maybe, in this case, it's the best thing that could have happened,' he said, his voice deep and warm. 'This has made me realise a thing or two about myself.'

'All the same, I don't think you're going to change a lot,' she told him demurely, as he tucked the wide folds of the oilskin about her. 'I don't see how I'm going to walk back like this,' she said with a little laugh. 'I feel rather like a well-wrapped Christmas parcel.'

'I think you've done enough walking,' he told her. 'I haven't the slightest intention of letting you take another step.'

As he spoke he turned off the light in the lantern and leaving it dangling on the branch of the tree he swept her up in his arms, holding her close and firmly.

'We shan't need the lantern,' he told her as he set off for the black house. 'I know every stick and stone of this terrain. And in fact I brought the lantern only because— well, I thought the light might be a—a sort of comfort to you.'

Her cheek pressed against the roughness of his jacket, Beverley smiled to herself. Was it possible that Alex was actually a little embarrassed that he had revealed the tender side of his nature?

She marvelled at his surefootedness over the stony branch-strewn ground. The wind blew as hard as ever, but he didn't even seem to be aware of it. And at that moment Beverley, safe and snug inside the folds of his cape, had no regrets that she had no bump of direction. After all, if she had never experienced this adventure they might never have been brought so closely together.

A little drowsily she wished that the return to Kinneil might be delayed, for, deep down, although she wouldn't actually acknowledge it to herself, there was a little pricking anxiety that she refused to admit. Alex would not change overnight. Nor did she want him to. It was impossible to tell what battles might take place between them in the future.

She was almost asleep as Alex placed her in the dinghy and they sped towards Kinneil. Like all the other houses on Kinneil the door of the guesthouse was left unlocked, and afterwards Beverley had only a hazy memory of being carried up to the house and of Alex pushing open the door.

In the parlour a peat fire glowed dully and as Alex placed her on the sofa she blinked her eyes and sat up. There was no sign of the sisters, but a note on the mantelshelf told them that a tasty supper had been left in the oven.

As he unwrapped the dripping oilskin, he said, 'Now pop up and get into something dry while I make things shipshape down here.'

With a little sigh of contentment Beverley climbed slowly upstairs. It was wonderful to have things taken completely out of her hands. Somehow she had never before felt this dependable comforting feeling in Alex's presence. The prickliness—for the time being at least—that usually existed between them had completely disappeared. And now his very presence gave her a warm sheltered feeling.

When she came down again it was in warm dry clothes. The fire had been built up and the flames roared up the chimney. An armchair had been pulled forward and in front of it was placed a basin of warm water.

As soon as he saw her Alex placed her firmly in the armchair, pulled off her slippers and placed her feet gently but firmly in the warm water.

As Beverley put up a weak protest, he said with mock severity, 'Do as you're told or you'll get no supper and, as far as I can make out, it's shepherd's pie and, as you know, Morag's is the best on the island. Well, what's the joke?' he demanded as he fetched a thick fluffy towel and placed it on the arm of her chair.

'It's simply that I never visualised you as the kind of man who fetches hot foot-baths for ladies in distress!'

'No? But then I don't think you know me very well,' he returned as he dried each foot slowly and put on her slippers once more.

'No, perhaps I don't,' she admitted, feeling a little taken aback at his brusque retort. 'But then I'm afraid you're a man who would take quite a lot of getting to know.' Immediately she regretted her words. They could so easily set off another storm and irrevocably spoil the moment of warm intimacy that linked them like a tender fragile chain.

Without answering and with the same quick deft movements Alex fetched a small fireside table. Then going to the kitchen he returned with two steaming plates of shepherd's pie. On the table he laid the cutlery and condiments in a slapdash manner that would certainly not have met with the approval of the MacCrimmon sisters. But Beverley gave a little sigh of contentment, feeling glad that the sisters were not there watching with amusement Alex's solicitude, and observing her reactions—and this after the many complaints she had made of Alex's bad behaviour.

She found herself saying a little shyly, 'It was good of you to come and rescue me.'

'You didn't really think I was going to leave you to spend the night in the woods, just because of a lost kit? It seems to me you'll have to readjust your thinking as far as I'm concerned, Beverley. I seem to appear to you as a sinister and frightening figure.'

'No, of course not,' she said hastily, 'but—but you're so used to the island yourself, I thought you might feel it would be fairly easy for me to find my way back to the black house no matter what part of the island I was in.'

'Although you appear to know very little about me, I know something about you, something I noticed right from the start.'

'Yes?' she queried, not knowing what to expect.

'That you're very definitely accident-prone,' he concluded rather squashingly, 'and that you've no bump of direction.'

'Oh!' she exclaimed, deflated.

'Why so disappointed? Did you expect a compliment?'

'I certainly shouldn't have expected one from you,' she replied, a little wistfully. Was he already tired of her adventure and perhaps regretting the pampering he had done? 'I'm sorry,' she said in a small voice. 'I'm afraid I've been an awful nuisance, haven't I?'

She leaned forward watching his face eagerly. For some reason she felt that his reply would be overwhelmingly important to her. But at that moment, to her dismay, the door opened and the MacCrimmon sisters came in.

CHAPTER EIGHT

WITH the arrival of the sisters the feeling of intimacy departed from the room. Alex was already filling his pipe and smiling slightly as he listened to the sisters' gossip.

'I see you've both enjoyed the shepherd's pie,' Morag said with satisfaction, as she gathered up the plates.

In an effort to cover the disappointment she felt at their presence, Beverley said lightly, 'A little more of your cooking, Morag, and I'll become enormous.'

'You could do with a few pounds,' Morag beamed, evidently gratified with the idea of Beverley growing fat on her culinary skills.

But Alex, as he lit his pipe said, without looking at her, 'I think Beverley's about perfect as she is. Slimness suits her, so perhaps we'd better keep her that way, Morag.'

'Nonsense!' Morag told him robustly. 'Just because you're one of those lean, rangy Highlanders there's no reason why Beverley shouldn't put on a pound or two. But not at present, for your dress is ready, Beverley. What about trying it on? I think you're going to like it.'

Beverley got to her feet eagerly. 'Oh, I'd just love to see it,' she said.

'Not tonight,' Alex put in quietly.

Beverley stared at him in astonishment. 'And why not?'

'Because it's late and you've already had enough excitement for one day. I suggest you pop up to bed and get a good sleep.'

Beverley opened her eyes wide. 'Really, who on earth do you think you are, Alex Ramage? Morag has gone to endless trouble making my dress and now you tell me not to try it on!'

'Perhaps he's right!' Morag's tone was conciliatory. 'You look quite worn out.'

'Well, I don't feel worn out,' Beverley said crossly. She had the curious feeling that should she let Alex get his own way concerning the dress it would be a subtle victory for him. Although, in spite of her brave words, she did indeed feel overwhelmingly tired.

Morag hesitated, looking from one to the other in indecision.

But Alex quietly and finally put an end to the altercation by saying, 'Tomorrow will be time enough. She won't be going over to Solan in the morning, and after she's had a good lie-in she can do all the primping she wishes.'

There was something so decisive about this pronouncement that Morag with a little shrug took the dishes out into the kitchen.

Fuming, Beverley got to her feet and marched from the room. So he was going to allow her a long lie-in, was he? Who did he think he was? She marched up to her room, her mind buzzing with retorts, feeling frustrated that it was now too late to throw them at him. Still resentful of Alex's autocratic behaviour, she undressed and got into bed in record time.

She had barely put her head on the pillow when she heard Alex's footsteps coming up the stairs. To her surprise he stopped outside her door, then after a slight hesitation, he knocked.

Beverley clamped her lips firmly together. Let him knock! she thought. She would maintain a discouraging silence.

Far from being defeated by this, he knocked several times more, and then coolly opened the door.

Before Beverley could close her eyes and feign sleep, she found herself held by that penetrating gaze of his that seemed to hold the cold of Northern climes.

'Just to remind you,' he informed her coolly, 'that to-morrow you mustn't attempt to get up. Have a long lie-in. You certainly need it after the alarms and excursions of the day.'

'Thanks!' she retorted coldly. 'But I've no intention of staying in tomorrow. There's no need for you to worry about me. I feel perfectly all right and I shall set off for work as usual.' She turned round and closed her eyes with an air of finality. But her ears were pricking as she waited for his departing footsteps.

But there was nothing but silence. And suddenly it seemed as if his presence permeated the whole room. How was it that this man had such a devastating effect on her? she wondered. His very silences seemed somehow full of significance.

Then, her eyes still tightly closed, she heard him say quietly, 'Tomorrow when I set off the tide will be in. I shan't take you with me, so don't bother to come down to the jetty. Later on, if you want to walk across, that's your own business.' And turning, he walked from the room.

When he had closed the door, Beverley sat up with a jerk. Alex Ramage was not going to treat her like a foolish child, she decided. She reached out and deliberately set her clock for early morning. Whether he liked it or not, she would be on the jetty in time to cross to Solan, and if he didn't like it he would have to remove her from the dinghy forcibly. But if he did—and she had a lurking suspicion that he might—at least she would have shown him that she was prepared to do a full day's work. She would show him that she was no fragile Victorian miss.

But Beverley was much more tired than she realized and in spite of the ringing alarm she slept late and awoke with a start to find the sun shining through her window.

She jumped out of bed, aware of all the sounds of late morning, and ran across to the window. There was no sign of the dinghy. Alex had gone without her. He had won, she thought chagrined. Somehow the idea of crossing to the island in the afternoon no longer appealed. This was something he had actually given her permission to do, and the very fact made her pout her lip obstinately. Probably he thought she would come running as soon as she was able to cross to Solan by foot. It might puzzle him just a little if she didn't turn up at the black house that day. She felt a faint glow of satisfaction at the thought.

There were plenty of things for her to do that morning. First of all there was the dress to discuss with Morag. There were letters home that she had neglected to write. Apart from that she decided to rest for a while on the swing lounge in the garden. And once she was there Isa might look for a bit of assistance with her plants. Yes, altogether she intended to have a most enjoyable time, a full day of relaxation, with the satisfying knowledge that her absence might just cause Alex a bit of consternation.

Morag entered with the dress over her arm. 'Well, you certainly had a good long sleep this morning! It was sensible of you to listen to Alex. I know he can be despotic at times, but he's usually right.'

'I certainly didn't intend to listen to him,' Beverley told her a little snappishly, 'but I didn't hear the alarm ring.'

'Well, never mind,' Morag said soothingly. 'It will be a

change for you to have some time off. And now you must try on the dress and tell me what you think of it.'

When Morag had helped her into it and she stood in front of the long mirror, she gave a little breathless gasp of pleasure. 'Oh, but it's beautiful, Morag!'

'Yes, it suits you to a T,' said Morag with satisfaction. 'It's all due to the exquisite silk. And the beauty of it is that Thai silk doesn't crush, so you need have no worries about that on the great night. Well, although I do say so, I think I have made a good job of it. It should certainly cause a sensation, for I doubt very much if even Lynne has ever worn such exquisite material.'

Beverley regarded herself in the mirror, speechless with surprise and pleasure. Morag was right. The beautiful ivory white material with its turquoise designs was perfect against her hair and skin.

Later on, when Morag had departed carefully carrying the dress wrapped in tissue paper, Beverley slipped into slacks and a light cashmere sweater. It was amazing what gorgeous plumage could do for a girl, she thought, as she gazed at herself now, looking rather young and schoolgirlish in her informal clothes. No longer was she the elusive beauty who had stared back at her a short time ago.

She spent the day very much as she had planned. And when she had helped Isa in the garden she fetched writing materials from her room and stretched out on the garden lounge gently swinging beneath the striped canopy while a salt-laden breeze stole in from the sea.

But by the afternoon she found her eyes straying towards the spot where Solan rested like a floating bouquet on the surface of the sea. No doubt by this time it had dawned on Alex that she wasn't coming, and she hoped it wasn't just wishful thinking that her absence might puzzle and perhaps trouble him a little.

She strolled into the village to send off some postcards and then returned to the swinging lounge with a paperback she had purchased. But gradually a nip came into the air as evening drew on and she decided to go into the house. She scanned the sea before getting up, realising with dismay how eagerly she was looking forward to his return. What a fool she was, to let her heart play such tricks on her at the first sight of those broad shoulders and the bony angular features. Love was such an unreasonable emotion, she thought disconsolately, without rhyme or reason. What had Alex Ramage above other men that set her heart racing and seemed to turn her whole life askew?

She picked up her book and wandered into the house. It would not be long until the evening meal. She would see him then.

But by the time she had helped Isa to lay the table and had helped Morag to dish up she realised that he had no intention of returning. His absence did not seem to surprise the sisters in the slightest. They were used to his staying on at Solan whenever he was involved in some particular piece of work that held his interest. Beverley dare not question them about his absence because she knew she would appear selfconscious no matter how casual she tried to appear. She felt bitterly disappointed, but made an effort to join in the gossip the sisters exchanged over the dining-table.

Eventually, when later that night she reached her bedroom, she found it impossible to settle down. Her mind ranged over the last interview she had had with him. After all, he had only displayed solicitude for her welfare, but she had as good as accused him of bullying her and had obstinately refused to fall in with his wishes. Then, when morning came, she had been so tired that she hadn't even heard the alarm. Which proved that Alex had been right when he had said that she needed to rest.

When he returned she would eat humble pie, she told herself. But not too obviously! By subtle means, she would let him know that she regretted her behaviour.

The long slow twilight of the Hebrides had filled her room with shadows. It was time to light the lamp if she was to while away the time by reading. But before doing so she crossed to the window and gazed out towards Solan, hoping to have a glimpse of it before it vanished like a mirage into the gathering dusk. Instantly her attention was caught by a boat moving across the water. A pale silvery moon had arisen and distinctly she saw Alex's tall, broad-shouldered figure. Then with a quickening of her senses she realised there was a woman with him. She had sheets of silky fair hair, shining silver in the light of the moon and was leaning forward eagerly as though chatting to her companion. It was Lynne Redfern, Beverley felt sure. But somehow she must find out for certain. Somehow it seemed dreadfully important that she should know who this woman was.

She caught up a lightweight coat, slipped down the stairs silently and stole through the garden. She wanted to get as near to the jetty as possible, But where to hide? There was a great clump of bushes near the path from the jetty, but she was nervous of concealing herself there. If she were to be discovered she would never be able to live down the shame of having spied on Alex. No, it was too dangerous. He had an amazingly quick ear and lightning quick movements, she had discovered.

Then she remembered the shed in which the furniture had been stored before they had taken it across to Solan. There was a small dusty window on the side near the path. Once inside she would be able to take stock of Alex's companion without being detected. She had to hurry to carry out her plan, because every moment was bringing the boat nearer. She ran along the little stretch of path that led to the shed and thrust her hand against the creaking door. As she pushed frantically, it gave way and she was able to slip inside and stand in the darkness gasping for breath.

Standing on tiptoe, she brushed some cobwebs from the window and stared out. She had a comprehensive view of the boat's arrival and she watched avidly as Alex tied up and helped his companion out. Then, arm in arm, they approached along the path.

When they were almost level with her hiding-place, Beverley's curiosity was satisfied. Yes, she had been right! Lynne Redfern was his companion, and from snatches of their conversation she gathered they had spent most of the day on Solan.

Listening, Beverley felt an overwhelming jealousy engulf her. It was an emotion she had always despised in others, but now she discovered with horror that she herself was its victim. How dared Lynne usurp her place at the black house! She visualised her taking possession. Making little sophisticated asides to Alex in her high silvery voice! Laughing at her efforts at home-making! The poised woman of the world pointing out to Alex the naïveté of his employee.

She was certain too that Alex would not treat this cool, self-possessed woman with the barely suppressed impatience he so often displayed to herself. No doubt they had conversed as equals and Alex, for once, had laid aside his studies in honour of his visitor.

They stopped for a moment almost opposite the shed and Beverley was forced to stoop down under the level of the window in case they should catch a glimpse of her. But she could hear what they were saying, in brief snatches. 'Poor Beverley's little treasures,' was one phrase she caught in Lynne's clear tones. Alex's voice, low and insistent, replied. She did not catch what he said, but again came Lynne's tones, 'Oh, very well, if you want it that way! Tomorrow, then. I'll see what I can do.' Then more loudly came the words, 'There's tonight, you know! It's not late for us at the Castle. Daddy and Mummy will welcome you for a nightcap, and the MacCrimmons will hardly try to lay down the law – not to you, if you come in late.'

Beverley got the impression that he hesitated, and when at last he did reply his voice was too low for her to catch his words. But there could be no mistaking the tone of triumph in Lynne's responding laugh.

She watched as together they walked towards Lynne's parked sports car.

For a long moment after the sound of their departure had faded, Beverley stood in the darkness, her nails biting into the palms of her hands, not realising that tears of frustration were pouring down her cheeks. With a woman's instinct she felt that Lynne's apparently casual invitation had been a premeditated move, a beautiful woman's conscious desire to exercise her power over a man as apparently unattainable as Alex!

When Beverley emerged from the shed and made her way across the garden she made no attempt to conceal her return to the house. What did it matter if the sisters spied her from their windows?

When at last she got into bed sleep eluded her. Subconsciously she was determined to stay awake, determined to discover exactly at what time he returned from his visit to Kinneil Castle. It seemed many hours later before she heard his footsteps ring on the road and recognised the tune he was softly whistling to himself as he came up to the door and let himself in. Then came the sound of his footsteps on the stairs and of his bedroom door shutting quietly.

It had been quite a prolonged nightcap, thought Beverley bitterly. Had Mr Redfern tactfully departed and left the couple to amuse themselves? It was hardly likely he had remained to act as chaperon to his very liberated daughter! At last, worn out with the conflicting emotions of the evening, Beverley fell into a sound sleep.

She awoke early on the following morning and was on the point of getting up when Isa came in with a breakfast tray. 'No need to stir, my dear,' Isa told her as she placed the tray across her knees. 'Alex says you're to take more time off if you feel like it.'

'Does he indeed?' Beverley returned through set teeth. 'How considerate of him! Well, he needn't worry. I shall go across to Solan this morning and you may be sure I shall turn in a full day's work. He doesn't think I'm going to lie in bed and collect my salary for doing nothing, does he?'

Isa looked a little startled at her vehemence. 'But, my dear, I'm sure he's only being considerate. Actually you should be rather flattered,' she added a little ruefully, 'because I can assure you he's not the sort of man who gives a lot of consideration to people as a rule.'

'Well, *I'm* not flattered,' Beverley returned, sitting upright and attacking her breakfast with a sort of suppressed fury.

Isa smiled. 'So you and he have been having a bit of a spat, is that it?'

'No, not exactly.' Suddenly Beverley felt deflated. I'm just suffering from an attack of the green-eyed monster, she thought as she buttered the crisp home-made bread. 'I suppose he hasn't left for Solan yet?' she asked anxiously. She had an overwhelming urgency to be on time, alert and ready for work. She would let Alex see that she was no malingerer.

As soon as she had finished breakfast she jumped out of bed and dressed as fast as she could, putting on slacks and a tee-shirt.

When she went downstairs she met Alex coming out of the parlour. He looked faintly surprised. 'I asked Isa to let you know that if you don't feel up to it there's no necessity for you to come over to Solan today.'

She assumed an artificial brightness and smiled cheerfully. 'But of course I feel up to it. Why shouldn't I? I mean, nothing terribly exciting has happened to me, has it?'

For a moment he frowned thoughtfully. 'No, I suppose not. Not from my point of view anyway. But then it's hard to know how a girl would feel about it.'

'Well, this girl doesn't feel a thing!' she assured him, still smiling broadly, 'so you can take that weight off your mind.'

His hazel eyes surveyed her shrewdly for a moment and then he nodded, as though realising the rancour that lay behind her attitude. 'I see! In that case there's nothing to keep us. We can start off immediately.' And, without waiting, he turned on his heel and strode out of the house and towards the jetty. Beverley found herself almost running to keep up with his long stride and it was in almost complete silence they crossed to Solan.

Once again Alex strode off and she found herself slipping and sliding as she traversed the boulders in his wake.

Instead of entering the house he went into the shed in which all sorts of odds and ends were stored. 'You may as well go on in!' he called over his shoulder as he began to rummage among a pile of implements.

Beverley did not reply, but gave him an indignant glare as she pushed open the door.

Then, as her eyes became accustomed to the dimness of the interior, she gave a little gasp of horror, for the room she had taken such pride in was almost unrecognisable. Everywhere was a scene of destruction. A couple of the gold and white cups the MacCrimmon sisters had given her lay shattered on the floor. The red plush armchair had been gashed by razor-sharp claws and the top of the table, which she had polished so carefully, was scratched and scored with livid furrows. The curtains too had not escaped. In places they looked as if they had been sliced through with a pair of sharp scissors, and she knew immediately that the kits, in one of their more playful moods, had used the curtains as a sort of ladder. In fact, the black house seemed to have been used as a sort of play-pen by those two destructive little animals. All the little touches she had added to make the house more attractive and habitable had been wiped out – and yet the two kits were safely in their boxes.

As she picked up her precious screen which was lying on its side, Alex came in. Beverley examined the screen anxiously, but apart from one or two loosened shells it seemed to be undamaged. 'The kits did this,' she said flatly. 'But how did they get out?' For at that moment the two cats were sitting demurely in the corners of their boxes looking the picture of innocence.

As she glanced at him she thought that for a moment she detected a look of discomfort, but immediately he turned away and picked up a few shards of broken china from the floor.

'But why did you let them go on like this?' she continued. 'Perhaps they escaped while you were out? Was that it?'

Again he didn't answer. And suddenly realisation swept over her and the black rage that she had felt in the shed on the previous night returned and enveloped her in a blinding miasma.

'It was Lynne, wasn't it?' she pronounced in a voice choked with fury. 'You took out the kits to show them to her and let them use the house as a sort of play-pen. No doubt she found it very amusing.'

As she spoke she could so easily visualise Lynne mocking at the little housewifely touches she had made to the black house.

'She asked to see them,' Alex said coolly. 'I left her playing with them. I was away only for a little, but I'm afraid she found them rather a handful and completely unmanageable. When I came in again the damage was done.'

'While you were away Lynne deliberately let them tear around destroying as much as possible,' she told him, her lips tight with rage. 'Why, it would take ages to set the place to rights,' she added, glancing about at the scene of chaos.

'Now you're talking nonsense!' he told her irritably. 'Remember this isn't the drawing-room of a Victorian mansion. It seems to me you've got a completely wrong idea of the sort of work that should be going on here. We're not playing at house, you know. If you're going to be all pie-faced about this, then you know what you can do!'

For a moment she glared at him, speechless with rage. Then, picking up one of the broken cups, she fired it at him with all her might.

But with a quick movement he sidestepped. It crashed into the wall behind him and shattered into tiny shards.

'You know, you're a rotten shot,' he told her coolly. 'If you hadn't lost your temper you might have taken proper aim and scored a bullseye.'

His coolness increased her bitterness. 'Yes, it was a pity to spoil one of "poor Beverley's little treasures", as Lynne calls them,' she retorted. 'But then Lynne never had to make do with the bits and pieces from the attics of the Guesthouse.'

While she was speaking a thoughtful frown was creasing his tanned forehead. 'By the way, what made you think it was Lynne who let the kits out?'

Beverley swallowed, the wind taken completely out of her sails as she realised how she had betrayed her knowledge that Lynne had been at Solan. 'Oh, I—I happened to see the boat returning to Kinneil. Lynne was with you.'

His lips tightened. 'That still doesn't explain how you heard Lynne speak about "poor Beverley's little treasures". You must have overheard her.'

She didn't reply.

'Well?' he demanded, his voice sharp and peremptory. 'Why don't you answer?' He considered her thoughtfully. 'To have heard that remark you must have been near the jetty, yet I saw no sign of you last night. Where were you?'

Beverley tried to keep her face as expressionless as possible. To show signs of guilt would be disastrous, she realised.

'Let's see now! You weren't hiding in the bushes, by any chance?'

The scorn in his tone pricked her into defensiveness. 'No, of course I wasn't!' she returned angrily.

'Well now, where else could you have been? Let's think. The only other place in which you would have been invisible and yet could have heard that remark is the shed.'

At his words Beverley knew that the guilt she felt was visible to his observant eyes.

'So you were hiding in the shed—eavesdropping,' he told her in a tone of such contempt that Beverley flared into angry self-defence.

'Don't dare speak to me in that manner!' she cried. 'Don't you think that what you did was rotten? To stand by, cool as you please, while Lynne let the kits destroy everything I've done here!'

'I shan't say anything about your remarks about myself,' he replied, 'but as far as Lynne is concerned, you're speaking as if she's some sort of monster who would deliberately destroy what you've established here. The truth is that what happened was a simple accident. How was she to know how troublesome the kits can be?'

'You're defending her!' cried Beverley, beside herself with anger. 'But anything is good enough for me! You've always treated me rottenly, Alex Ramage, and now you've nerve enough to say if I don't like it I know what I can do. Well, I *don't* like it, and I'm not going to stand it one moment longer. You can clear up this mess yourself if you want to, because I shall never set foot in this house again—never, never!'

Before he could reply to this she whirled about and darted out of the house.

CHAPTER NINE

RAGE carried her across the island on winged feet. She made her way through the boulders that fringed the shore without the smallest difficulty. But when she came to the water's edge she hesitated. The tide was not yet completely out, but she could not possibly ask Alex for the use of the boat. Throwing caution to the winds, she plunged in, and found that luck favoured her. At no place was the channel deeper than knee-high, but by the time she stepped ashore in Kinneil she was dripping wet and feeling thoroughly chilled and exhausted. As she staggered along the beach only the thought of the MacCrimmons' cosy parlour with its glowing fire and steaming cups of strong tea gave her the impetus to carry on to the door.

As she entered the parlour the sisters looked up, startled and dismayed by her appearance. Her eyes were wide and dark, water dripped on to the carpet from her drenched clothes and as she found the sisters gazing at her in blank astonishment Beverley, in spite of all her efforts, burst into tears.

But at last, dry, and seated by the fire with a piping hot cup of tea, she felt sufficiently recovered to relate her tale of woe. Dramatically she ended her recital with the words. 'And so I told him I wasn't going to work with him again! The best thing for me to do would be to go home immediately.'

She waited, confident of the sisters' approbation. But, to her dismay, her outburst was followed by a long and disapproving silence.

Recovering her voice, Morag said, 'But, my dear, you can't mean that! Remember there are other people involved in this! If you go immediately you'll miss the ball. Think of all the trouble I've gone to about your dress. To be quite frank, I was counting on it being noticed. The Redferns have so many wealthy friends! If I could get a few orders it would make all the difference to Isa and myself, especially during the winter months when we have no visitors staying with us.'

'I'm sorry!' Beverley told her, a little resentfully. 'And I'm really not ungrateful. But it's completely impossible for me to work with Alex now. I thought you'd see my point of view,' she added, feeling thoroughly sorry for herself.

'Well, frankly, dear, no,' Isa supported her sister. 'Was the damage so very serious that you must take such a strong line?' As Beverley's eyes widened in amazement, Isa went on quickly, 'After all, the furniture was the sort of thing people keep in their attics. Everything can easily be replaced. But to leave, just in the middle of Alex's work—well, it doesn't seem to me to be doing the fair thing by him!'

Beverley felt a great wave of self-pity flow over her. Everyone was against her, it seemed—Alex, Lynne Redfern, and now the MacCrimmons, whom she had felt so sure she could depend on if it came to a showdown with Alex.

'I suppose I did rather lose my temper,' she agreed rather tartly, 'but I must say I think I had good cause.'

As she spoke there flashed into her mind the moment when she had thrown a teacup at him, and she was glad this was something the sisters did not know about. It was only too easy to imagine their tight-lipped disapproval of the incident.

'It seems to me you're taking the whole thing far too seriously,' Isa went on in her usual comfortable voice. 'After all, the damage can be repaired, and you must remember that, unreasonable as it may seem to you, the kits are part of Alex's work. Everything is of secondary importance to it, as far as he's concerned. After all, you knew what you were taking on when you accepted this job.

Alex's studies involve dealing with wild creatures, and you must take the rough with the smooth.'

'Apart from the fact that he *is* your boss!' Morag added dryly.

Beverley felt a growing resentment. It was only too clear where the MacCrimmons' loyalty lay. She was being made to appear mulish and unreasonable. 'I don't see why *I* should be put in the wrong,' she began sullenly.

'Not in the wrong, dear,' Isa told her gently. 'Simply that you're rather hot-tempered, I think. I can only suggest that you make up with him immediately.'

'I'm sure, if you think it over, you'll realise it's the best thing to do in the circumstances,' Morag put in firmly.

'You mean, I should apologise to him?' Beverley asked incredulously.

Morag nodded. 'Something like that! There are ways and means of letting a man know you've decided to climb down—without actually eating too much humble pie. Underneath Alex's steely exterior, he's like any other man and likes to be got around—especially by a pretty girl like you.'

But Beverley was not to be mollified. She set her jaw mulishly. 'Well, I'm not going to give him the satisfaction of trying to "get round" him! Why should I behave like some docile, downtrodden Victorian governess, just to soothe his masculine vanity? Anyway, even if I did get round him—which I don't intend to do—I still wouldn't go to the ball with him anyway!' And she turned and rushed from the room, banging the door behind her.

She was on the point of racing upstairs to the privacy of her bedroom when the front door opened and Lynne walked into the hall. For a moment the two girls stared at each other, and Beverley was aware that her own gaze was antagonistic.

'Where's Alex?' Lynne demanded.

For a moment Beverley was disconcerted. From the

scraps of conversation she had overheard on the previous evening she had imagined that Lynne's rendezvous was to be with Alex on Solan. 'He's on Solan, of course,' she replied when she had recovered herself.

There was silence for a few moments, then, with just a hint of self-consciousness, Lynne said, 'I gather from your manner that you've seen the black house?'

'Yes, I've seen it,' Beverley said tightly.

Lynne gave a little trill of uneasy laughter. 'So the cat's out of the bag—in every sense of the words.'

'I can't imagine why you've bothered to come and tell me this,' Beverley told her.

'Oh, this is Alex's doing!' Lynne returned, recovering her assurance. 'He's been nagging me to remedy some of the damage. We've all sorts of odds and ends here and there about the Castle. I could supply anything you want. I promised Alex I'd do it. I told him I'd call over today and find out exactly what you need.'

'Oh!' was all Beverley could find to say. So this was the meaning of the remarks she had overheard on the previous evening! The wind had been taken out of her sails. She hesitated, then said awkwardly, 'Thanks. I'll make up a list and let you have it.'

'Good!' Lynne replied briskly. 'I'll get them sent over right away.'

When Lynne had gone, Beverley slowly mounted the stairs. So she had let her senseless jealousy ruin everything between Alex and herself, she thought dismally. And now it was too late. She could not go to him and admit it had all been a hideous mistake. And now that she had told him she was leaving she couldn't possibly renege. To do so would put her in a horrible and contemptible position. Only too easily could she imagine his sardonic expression were she weakly to remain.

It would be a couple of days before the *Maid of the Islands* arrived on its tour of the islands, and for those days she was careful to avoid Alex. There were two dangerous moments in the day—in the mornings, before he left for Solan, and again in the evenings when he returned to Kinneil. But it was soon evident that he was just as anxious that they shouldn't have any encounters. Instead of returning for the evening meal, he remained on Solan till all hours. Beverley had gone to her room for the night before she heard the sound of the outboard motor put-puttering across the water. She would strain her ears for the sound of his footsteps in the hall and the deep tones of his voice as he spoke with Isa or Morag.

She passed part of those last two days in giving the sisters as much help as she could in preparing the house for their summer visitors. But she soon had to admit to herself that there was very little she could do to assist them, for the sisters worked as a well-co-ordinated team. A few concentrated hours each morning and they had the house shining and in apple-pie order. In the afternoons Isa would go into the garden and begin pottering amongst the flowerbeds.

It was Isa who suggested rather diffidently that Beverley should go to Alex and ask for her job back, for Lynne's offer to replace the damaged furniture had come to her ears. It was clear that the sisters considered her obstinate and pigheaded not to reciprocate in some way.

But the dress that Morag had made for her with such care was a subject too thorny to be referred to. Morag packed it safely away and it was never mentioned by either sister. The knowledge that to them she appeared ungrateful only added to Beverley's burdens. She began to spend most of her time in her room.

One of her most unpleasant tasks was writing home to her family to let them know that her adventures in the Hebrides were over. In previous letters she had told them how happy she was in her work and how well she was getting along with the sisters at the Guesthouse. They were sure to be puzzled by this complete about-face and the news that she was about to depart abruptly.

Her letter finished at last, she decided she would take a walk into the village to post it. She slipped on a sports coat and pushed the letter into the wide pocket. For a while she strolled about idly, putting off the moment when she would have to post her letter, and it happened that chance brought her near the pier. There were only a few idlers about, and she was surprised to catch sight of the Redferns' station waggon, and what was more, Lynne herself, who was busy stowing it with big cardboard boxes piled on the pier. Some of these looked rather heavy while others were bulky, and ordinarily Beverley would have gone forward to lend a hand, but after her recent set-to with the girl she didn't like to offer her help.

She had misjudged Lynne, Beverley was thinking, undecided about how she should behave now. It was true it was Lynne's fault that the black house had been devastated, but it was also true that no one but Alex himself could manage the kits. The damage that had been done was almost more his fault than Lynne's. And then Lynne had been generous in her offer to restore things as much as possible. No, the whole situation in which she now found herself was due to her own seething jealousy, Beverley was thinking with a leaden heart.

She took a deep breath and before she could change her mind, moved quickly forward and caught up an end of a particularly big box that Lynne was trying to lift into the station waggon.

'This is really sweet of you,' Lynne said a little breathlessly when at last they had angled it into place. 'Would you believe it, I sent a man down for these things this morning and he came back forgetting all about them! If you want a thing done you'd better do it yourself, it seems. These are Chinese lanterns. I thought they might look rather pretty strung among the bushes. Then I had to order extra glasses and china. Such numbers come, you see. They always do. In fact, everyone round about seems to turn up.

But then I don't mind admitting that we do things rather well,' she added complacently.

Together they stowed Lynne's purchases in the big car until it was almost completely loaded. Last of all remained a huge box. As it was rather heavy the two girls lifted it between them. 'Material for new drapes,' Lynne informed Beverley as they placed it in the only remaining space. 'It struck me that our old red ones looked rather dreary, so I went to Edinburgh and picked this stuff. We have a wonderful little woman who mends and does simple dressmaking, and I'm hoping she'll take on the job. Simply miles and miles of sewing! I must have been mad to think of it so late in the day when the ball is almost upon us, but the material is so pretty I simply couldn't resist it. It's a sort of oyster and pale lemon stripe.'

As she slid behind the wheel, she leaned out. 'Really, Beverley, you've been wonderful! I don't know what I should have done without you. I only wish I could talk Alex into lending you to me for a while—at least until the ball is over, but it's all a dream, of course.'

She smiled to show that this was intended only as a compliment and the thought passed through Beverley's mind with a little start of surprise that Alex had not told Lynne of the breach between them and of the fact that she no longer worked for him.

'And that brings me to something I want to say,' Lynne went on. 'It's about what happened at the black house, and how awful I feel about what happened. It looked so perfectly wonderful when George and I went across to see the kits—what with the charming pieces of bone china and the curtains on the window. You made the curtains yourself, didn't you?'

Beverley nodded wordlessly, uncertain how to receive Lynne's rather gushing compliments. It was Lynne's way, she was discovering, to speak in this fashion, so that it was difficult to discover when she was sincere and when she intended nothing more than a piece of civil flattery. But she felt sure that on this occasion Lynne was sincere in wishing to have her assistance in the preparations for the ball. And why not? she was thinking. If she no longer worked for Alex then she was free to take up any offer that came her way.

She drew a deep breath. 'Alex will be able to spare me all right,' she said. 'You see, I'm no longer working for him.'

Lynne looked taken aback. 'He didn't mention it to me,' she said a little tightly. Then immediately a look of triumph flashed into her green eyes. But what she said was, 'But that's terrible! What on earth happened?' Then without waiting for a reply, she went on, 'I know Alex can be perfectly obnoxious at times. But then he can be so attractive when he puts his mind to it that he usually gets away with it. You don't blame me any more for what happened at the black house?' she went on. 'But then I can see you don't. You know Alex was more to blame than I was. He shouldn't have left them with me knowing, as he must, how positively devilish the kits can be.' '

'You're right,' Beverley nodded. 'When you come to think of it, it was far more Alex's fault than yours. But then,' she added bitterly, 'Alex never did appreciate all the work I put into the house. In fact he rather dislikes it! Why, he actually had nerve enough to say I was behaving as if it was the drawing-room of a Victorian mansion.'

'What a perfectly hideous thing to say!' Lynne commiserated. She turned her head away and gazed out over the misty blue sea, and again in the depth of those beautiful eyes could be seen that gleam of triumph.

But Beverley was past observing such things. It felt wonderful to have found someone at last who would listen to her grievances. She found herself telling Lynne of Alex's cutting remarks, his overbearing ways, and when, at last, she came to a halt feeling rather foolish, Lynne said soothingly, 'Yes, the man's a perfect boor. At other times he can charm the birds out of the trees. *I* know. I *ought* to. After all, I think I'm the only woman in the world who really and truly understands him. He's inclined to ride roughshod over anyone who's soft enough to take it from him. *I* don't, of course, and I do believe that that's what attracts him to me. He admires people who are able to stick up for themselves.'

She regarded Beverley interestedly. 'But what are you going to do now?'

'Go home, I suppose,' Beverley admitted miserably. 'I loved it here, and I must say I was happy doing the work on Solan, and would have been perfectly willing to stay on, but—well, some of the things Alex said were unforgivable. I did think of working with the MacCrimmons, helping during the summer in the Guesthouse, I mean, but they don't really need me. They're well able to manage on their own. I suppose the only thing for it's to go home as soon as possible, because I must look out for another job.'

For a moment Lynne drummed her fingers thoughtfully on the wheel. 'You know, you could stay on here, at least until after the ball is over.'

Beverley looked at her enquiringly.

'I mean, you could take me up on the suggestion I made a few minutes ago. Would you consider helping me out with the preparations for the ball? It could be rather fun, you know. You could help me in all sorts of ways. I mean, you're very artistic! Look at what you made of the black house! And at the Castle, I can assure you, your efforts would be appreciated. Of course we've all sorts of help, but for the special effects you'd be invaluable. You could take over the arrangement of the flowers. I'm certain you would be wonderful at that, and it bores me stiff. Then there's the buffet. We're having caterers, of course, but they do need a touch of direction when it comes to making the supper-room presentable. Would you believe it, last year they could think of nothing better than shepherd's tartan.' When Beverley looked at her enquiringly, Lynne added, 'You know, that dismal black and white one. The effect was quite disastrous. And then one can't really trust the servants with our extra-special china. Mummy's always nervous if it isn't in the best of hands.'

As Beverley listened she found herself more and more taken by the idea. No doubt the inside of the Castle would be as attractive as its exterior. It would be interesting to get a taste of such gracious living. Apart from that, as Lynne had said, it sounded rather fun.

'Then there are the lanterns to be strung,' Lynne continued. 'Not that you would have to do that,' she laughed, 'but I'm sure you could direct the men to hang them in the most effective spots.'

Yes, she definitely would enjoy that sort of work, Beverley thought with satisfaction.

'Well, how do you feel about it? If you don't want to make up your mind immediately you could think it over and let me know.'

'I don't need to think it over,' Beverley told her. 'I've made up my mind. I'd like the job very much. And it's good of you to think of me,' she added a little haltingly, still feeling slightly ill at ease and on her guard.

But there could be no doubting that Lynne was pleased. 'Good,' she said briskly. 'What do you say we start tomorrow?'

Beverley nodded. 'Yes, I'd love that! And this means I shall be able to tell the MacCrimmons I shall be staying on.'

When Lynne had driven off, she raced back to the Guest-house, bubbling over with the news of her new job.

Again she burst in on them, but this time her face was glowing. 'Guess what!' she said excitedly. 'I was in the village, and who do you think I met but Lynne Redfern! And guess what?' She stopped dramatically.

The sisters shook their heads smilingly.

'She's offered me a job at the Castle, and it sounds absolutely wonderful. Marvellous things, like arranging the flowers and washing the most precious china! It will be a nice change from working at the black house,' she added a little defiantly.

To her surprise, the sisters' smiles faded and they glanced at each other covertly. She looked from one to the other. 'What's wrong? Don't you think it's a good idea?'

Morag hesitated, then said carefully, 'I think it's only fair to warn you that, charming as Lynne can be, she's changeable. She's been terribly spoilt by her parents, you know.'

'But what has that got to do with my job?' Beverley asked, puzzled.

'Well, we've heard stories from people who've worked for her in previous years, and quite frankly they say she can be a bit of a tartar.'

'But she was so nice, so friendly!' Beverley protested. 'She said all sorts of complimentary things about how artistic I am—that sort of thing. And about how helpful I'd be. What reason could she have but that she wanted to be friendly?'

'Beverley dear,' Isa put in gently, 'so far you've seen only one side of Lynne. Working for her will be a very different proposition. I mean, it all sounds very nice and the work appears light, but Lynne can be moody and can be quite unendurable at times!'

For a moment Beverley felt completely deflated. All her enthusiasm seemed to drain away as she heard the sisters' pessimistic prognostications. 'It would have meant I could have stayed on here,' she said disappointedly. 'Anyway,' she added more cheerfully, 'the job is only going to last until after the ball, so no matter how bad things are they're not going to last long. But I'm certain you're mistaken about Lynne. She really couldn't have been more charming.'

'Perhaps you're right,' Morag agreed without conviction. 'She may be on her best behaviour with you. Anyway, it will be wonderful having you staying on with us, so I can't say I'm sorry you took her up on it.'

'Yes, it's nice that you'll be able to stay on,' Isa put in.

'And maybe things will straighten out between you and Alex. It was sad to think you were parting on such bad terms.'

'It won't make any difference,' Beverley told her a little sadly. 'Alex will never forgive me for some of the things I said to him. I was in such a rage and—well, I said more than I meant to. But he was just as bad,' she added in a burst of indignation. 'He can be horribly arrogant and high-handed at times.'

'Yes, and he knows it too!' Morag told her. 'That's why, if you would only make the first move, I'm perfectly certain he would forgive and forget.'

Beverley shook her head. 'No, I simply couldn't. I'm certain he would just stop me off short, and I simply couldn't bear it.' Besides, she was thinking—although she did not say this to the MacCrimmons--if he should reject her efforts at reconciliation now she would never be able to offer him the olive branch later on.

'Anyway,' she said brightly, 'this new job of mine will mean I can wear something nice for a change and get out of jeans and a sweater. I think I'll go straight up,' she told them with a smile, 'and look out something suitable, something that will look right at Castle Kinneil.'

With her usual impetuosity she swung around and walked swiftly from the room, only to find herself colliding with Alex in the small hall. Too late, she spun around, her hand stretched out to prevent herself striking against the wall.

A moment later she found his arms about her, holding her securely. Surprise held her motionless for a long moment, then as she felt her heart thudding against his in the warm haven of his arms she pulled herself back with a sharp movement, and glared up at him.

'And just what do you think you're doing?' she demanded angrily.

'Preventing you from making a nasty hole in the wall,' he told her coolly.

'I was perfectly all right,' she snapped.

'In that case perhaps I'd better release you,' he said equably.

'Thanks, but I've already released myself,' she told him. Her eyes were hostile, but his held a sardonic amusement. She bit her lip as she swung around and darted up the stairs, aware that his eyes were following her.

Inside her room she leaned against the door, breathless. Why had she been so agitated by the small encounter when, only such a short time ago, she had been resigned to leaving Kinneil for ever? How dreadful to feel that Alex had a hold on her heart that nothing could break!

Her thoughts were still in a tumult as she swung open the door of her wardrobe and reached in for her favourite dress. As the work Lynne had outlined was so light and clean, she decided to wear it. It was in a thin filmy material in woodland tones of fawn, brown and leaf green, eminently suitable, she thought, for her new duties at Kinneil Castle.

On the following morning, at the sisters' suggestion, she went by the coast road, revelling in the salty tang of the sea as it broke on the boulders and in the scent from the masses of wildflowers that grew in the machair. Blue mountains were to the left of her and the white cottages of the crofters stood out like dolls' houses on the hillsides.

The Castle stood on a slight rise so that Beverley had a good view of it long before she reached the huge iron gates. It looked out over the sea. What an exquisite view there must be from those pepperpot towers, she thought as she slipped through the gates which stood ajar and walked up the long drive. On either side were great clumps of rhododendron with many other flowering shrubs, and as she rounded a slight bend she caught a glimpse of Mungo.

As soon as he caught sight of her he ran towards her, his short legs trotting as fast as he could. He jumped up and down, barking joyfully, his round bright eyes peering through fringes of white fluffy hair as she bent down to snuggle him in her arms.

Lynne must be somewhere about in the grounds, she was thinking as she walked on with the little dog in her arms. As the avenue opened up she found herself in front of the Castle with its long turrets, looking rather like a castle in 'Snow White'. Then she saw Lynne come towards her across the grass from the direction of a cluster of glasshouses that lay at a little distance.

'Oh, there you are!' Lynne exclaimed. 'I was wondering where Mungo had got to.'

'He is a dear.' said Beverley, as reluctantly she put him down.

But he stayed by her side, and Lynne called him a little crossly. It was with some backward glances at Beverley that he at last trotted off to join his mistress.

'It's just like a castle in a fairy-tale!' Beverley said admiringly, as she surveyed the scene, 'The walls are so white!'

'That's because they're harled,' Lynne informed her.

'Harled?'

'Yes, the walls are dressed with crushed sea-shells. That's what gives that effect of blinding whiteness.' It was evident she took pride in this Scottish home of hers. 'But you must come in and I'll show you around,' she offered pleasantly.

CHAPTER TEN

LYNNE led the way into an enormous hall from which lancet-shaped doors opened. High on the white walls were stags' heads and clusters of claymores. There was a wonderful ancient targe above the enormous chimneypiece of carved stone which stood at the far end of the great room. In the centre of a long table of oak was a beautiful silver quaich in which was displayed great pale pink hothouse carnations.

'That's the famous Kinneil quaich, isn't it?' Beverley asked eagerly as she gently touched the glowing cup with its two protruding handles.

'Yes, one of our heirlooms,' Lynne said with a little laugh. 'Not that any of the things here really belong to us—not as heirlooms anyway. Everything belongs to the previous owners. When Dad bought it, he took everything, lock, stock and barrel. But we've been lucky and have come in for some wonderful antique pieces.'

'It must be wonderful, having such romantic surroundings,' Beverley told her as they continued their tour of the Castle.

'Yes, it's wonderful,' Lynne agreed indifferently. 'I enjoy it for a while, I must say, but frankly I couldn't endure to remain all the year round. I get just about enough of it by the time the ball is over, and then I'm all ready to go back to town. But come, I must show you the ballroom. That's where I'm putting up the new curtains.'

As she spoke she pushed open one of the great iron-studded doors, and to Beverley's delight it gave a ghostly creak as it swung back. There was a short flight of curving stairs leading downwards into the huge room with its gleaming floor. The walls were of wood panelling painted silver. But what intrigued Beverley most was the mock minstrels' gallery of fretted wood.

Immediately Beverley's eyes went to a great pile of material striped in pale oyster and lemon yellow. So this was the fabric for the new curtains which Lynne had mentioned when they had met on the pier! 'This should look wonderful against the silver walls,' Beverley remarked.

'Yes, I do think I made a good choice,' Lynne agreed complacently. Nevertheless a frown creased her smooth brow as she regarded the great pile of material, and for a moment Beverley wondered what it was that had annoyed her.

Later she was to discover the answer to the niggling little

problem, but that was after she had been shown nearly every part of the Castle. There was so much to admire—the great elaborate four-poster beds which had been brought over from Holland in the seventeenth century. There was the room which Beverley preferred to all the others. This was a study which Lynne told her was a replica of the one used by Sir Walter Scott at Abbotsford. From it an enchanting spiral staircase rose to a comfortable bedroom above.

'It seems Sir Walter Scott used to come down from his bedroom in the early mornings and put a light to his study fire and set to work writing his novels, long before anyone else in the house was about,' Lynne told her. 'But why Daddy had this built, I don't know, because I don't suppose he's ever put a light to a fire in his life, nor would he dream of climbing a spiral staircase to his bedroom.'

By some twisting turret stairs she led Beverley to an upper storey of the Castle. 'Mrs McKendrick, our sewing woman, has a room here, and I may as well ask her about the curtains now.' Again Beverley noticed that slight frown of displeasure.

This upper storey of the Castle was in contrast to the rest of the building: the rooms seemed shabby and rather down-at-heel. It was clear that at one time this had been the sleeping quarters of the staff. The room in which Beverley now found herself contained a long scarred work table and an ancient sewing-machine.

A small, rather sour-faced woman was cutting material at the table as they entered. She looked up briefly and unsmilingly continued with her work.

'Ah, Mrs McKendrick, busy as usual, I see!' Lynne said brightly in what Beverley designated her lady-of-the-castle voice.

'Ah thought ye kent I was always busy!' replied Mrs McKendrick snappishly. 'These sheets are in a bad way. Almost wore out, if you ask me.'

'Actually,' Lynne smiled tightly, 'it's not the linen I'm so worried about, it's the drapes. I see you haven't taken the material up. You'd have to get started immediately, you know, or we won't have the ballroom ready in time.'

Mrs McKendrick laid down her scissors and pursuing her lips ominously turned and faced Lynne. 'I may as well tell you here and now,' she informed her, 'that I haven't any intention of making up those drapes. You knew what length those ballroom windows are! The drapes are going to weigh about a ton, and if you think I'm going to run them up on that old sewing-machine you've another think coming.'

Lynne raised her eyebrows. 'Really, there's no need to be offensive!' she snapped. 'I know the drapes are going to be a heavy job, but it's a pity you didn't even make a start on them.'

Mrs McKendrick snorted aggressively. 'I never begin what I don't mean to finish,' she said shortly. 'And I'm not going to do those drapes—you can make your mind up for it!' And turning away, she picked up her scissors and began to snap viciously at a length of linen.

For once Lynne appeared irresolute and Beverley got the impression that she had realised that the sewing-woman was obdurate. She swung about and, followed by Beverley, walked in an affronted manner from the room. As she led the way down the turret stairs she said over her shoulder, 'Mrs McKendrick can be very changeable, you know! To think that she's actually cut the drapes, and now refuses to run them up! If I had my way I'd simply let her go, but Mummy thinks highly of her, so——' Dismissing the subject, as they reached the hall, she added, 'Well, now that you've seen most of the Castle I suggest we get to work.'

'What would you like me to do?' Beverley asked, as Lynne paused thoughtfully.

Again Lynne hesitated. 'You've seen how completely

pigheaded Mrs McKendrick is about the drapes', she began. 'Do you think, Beverley, there's any chance you could run them up for me?' Then, seeing the expression of dismay that flashed into Beverley's face, she added quickly, 'Oh, I don't mean all at once, you know. But perhaps you could make a start this morning. After lunch you could do something quite different by way of a change.'

Without waiting for Beverley's reply, she glanced at her watch. 'I've loads of things to do this morning. You know where the ballroom is now, don't you? Could you take the material up to the sewing-room and tell Mrs McKendrick she can have the rest of the day off? That should mollify her, I should imagine.' And before Beverley could utter a protest, she turned away and crossed the hall with her long graceful swinging stride.

When Mrs McKendrick had departed, not mollified, but in a flurry of indignation, Beverley applied herself to the task of threading the ancient machine with thread to match the drape material. When at last she got it clanking she laboured up the turret stairs with the first of the material, and set to work.

It was with a sigh of relief that she heard the luncheon gong sound. She stood up, her arms aching with feeding the heavy rich material under the needle of the old sewing-machine.

When she reached the hall Lynne was waiting for her. She looked cool and fresh while Beverley was only too well aware that she looked the complete opposite.

'Poor Beverley,' Lynne remarked, 'you look all worn out. I hope you haven't been working too hard.'

'The machine *is* rather ancient,' Beverley told her mildly.

'Yes, I know,' Lynne agreed. 'And I meant to ask Mummy and Daddy to order a new one, but I forgot all about it this morning. The parents are off for a jaunt about the mainland. They left on the *Maid of the Islands* this morning. Anyway, the old machine will do until after the ball, won't it, and a good lunch will restore you, I hope.'

Tucking her arm through Beverley's, she led her into a small room, surprisingly cosy with chintz drapes and chair coverings, in contrast to the rather bleak splendour of the rest of the Castle. 'This will give us the chance to have a cosy chat, heart to heart, having lunch together, just the two of us,' Lynne remarked as they seated themselves at a small round table set with gleaming china and snowy damask.

Beverley's dormant suspicions of Lynne immediately rose to the surface. 'A cosy chat about what?' she asked cautiously.

'About what your plans are, after you finish here, I mean,' Lynne replied without hesitation. 'Are you going back home? Or is it that after you've let sufficient time pass and he's cooled down, you intend to stage a big reconciliation scene with Alex?'

'Now just what do you mean by that?' Beverley demanded sharply. 'There's not the smallest chance of my staging a "reconciliation scene", as you call it.'

'Dear me, you are prickly!' Lynne laughed. 'It's just that—well, now that we're getting to know each other a little better, naturally I'm interested in your future plans. I do feel it would be useless for you to try to patch things up with Alex. He can be quite ruthless at times. You can take my word for it, because I think I know him better than anyone else. Actually we're very close, Alex and I, although I admit he's not the openly demonstrative type. But then I rather like my men to be strong and silent,' she added lightly.

So Lynne was conveying the message, hands off Alex Ramage! And, with a little stab of pain, Beverley wondered just how close they were. But Lynne had been right when she described Alex as 'strong and silent'. He was certainly not the type of man who would kiss and tell.

Seeing that her message had got across to Beverley, Lynne adroitly turned the conversation to other subjects and soon they were discussing plans for the rest of the day. The meal was delicious and daintily served, and Beverley felt refreshed by the time it was over, and ready to begin her next task.

'You can leave the drapes until tomorrow,' Lynne told her. 'But I was wondering if, in the meantime, you'd go across to the glasshouses and ask old Tam to let you have a pot of those gorgeous pink azaleas he grows. I'd like to experiment with different colour combinations so that later on I'll know what will look best.'

Glad to escape from the gloomy sewing-room, Beverley crossed the grounds to the glasshouses. Tam, she discovered, was a gnome-like old man wearing a tartan tammy surmounted by a red pom-pom. She was rather taken aback by the pot he picked out for her. No doubt it was his prize specimen, because it was an enormous plant bearing clusters of beautiful pale pink blossoms, but it was heavy. As she tried to pick it up he said, 'I doubt you'll be able to carry it yourself. I'll have young Jimmy take it across to the house for you.'

'Oh, I'm sure I'll be able to manage,' Beverley said quickly. She suspected that Lynne would resent it if she returned to the house attended by one of the Castle employees. She had been told to fetch the plant and she was determined to do as she had been directed.

She seized the pot with all her might and somehow or other managed to convey it across the grounds and into the hall. As she put it down on the floor she could hear Lynne's voice speaking on the phone which was in an alcove off the hall. 'But is there no *message* for me?' she was asking irritably. There was a short silence and a moment later Lynne put down the receiver.

Her phone conversation had not been to her liking, Beverley realised as Lynne joined her, her expression stormy. 'Dear me, you *have* been a time,' she remarked. 'Now, let me see. Put it over there by the stairs so that I can get a good look at it.'

Exerting all her strength, Beverley picked up the pot again and placed it where she had been directed.

Lynne considered it, her lips pursed consideringly. 'Um, I'm not altogether happy, now that I actually see it here. In the glasshouse it looked so pretty, but here—well, it's a bit insipid, don't you feel that, Beverley?'

Beverley, who thought that the pale blossoms looked exquisite against the dark wood of the staircase, muttered something noncommittal.

But it was quite clear that Lynne was not really interested in her opinion, for she immediately added, 'I think you should trot back to Tam and say I'd prefer the dark crimson. I think, on the whole, it would be more suitable.' And without waiting for Beverley's reaction, she turned and walked swiftly out of the hall.

Once more Beverley picked up her load and somehow or other managed to get it back to the hothouse.

When she arrived, Tam, looking more than ever like an enraged gnome, fixed her with a baleful eye. 'No need to tell me!' he began. 'Her ladyship doesnae like this one. She wants something else.'

'I'm afraid that's so,' Beverley told him a little ruefully. 'It's the colour, you see. She's not very keen on the pale pink. I think she'd prefer one of the red.'

The pot he indicated was only slightly smaller than the one she had returned, and this time when he suggested that Jimmy should carry it to the house she agreed with alacrity.

Jimmy, smiling broadly with pleasure in being released even for a little while from the gnome's tyranny, led the way bearing the pot in his strong young arms. But as he reached the hall his smile faded when Lynne, catching sight of him, instantly demanded, 'What are you doing here, Jimmy? You should be working with Tam just now shouldn't you?'

'But it was Tam told me to carry the pot for the young lady,' Jimmy protested, abashed at Lynne's cold anger.

'Then he had no right to!' Lynne told him. 'When I asked Miss Nesbitt to fetch a pot, I didn't expect to see you arrive on the scene.'

Beverley bit her lip as she heard Lynne's biting acid tones.

When Jimmy had scuttled away Lynne regarded the crimson azalea for a long minute, then said to Beverley in a totally altered tone, 'You know, Beverley, now that I see it I'm not really so keen on azaleas after all. What I'd really like would be snow-white cyclamen. I feel it would look so much more dramatic. And we must remember that the whole affair will take place in electric light.'

Again she regarded the crimson azalea, her head on one side, then she said, in the friendliest possible manner, 'I hate giving you so much trouble, Beverley, but if it wouldn't be too much of a nuisance could you possibly take it back again and ask Tam if he could let us have something pure white. I'd have asked Jimmy to take this back if I'd realised in time that it wouldn't do.'

'Of course!' Once again Beverley picked up the pot. She found Lynne's sudden changes of mood bewildering and wondered which was the real Lynne. But she knew that Lynne had many friends—especially men friends—and wondered if it was this very changeableness which made her so fascinating. If that is her secret then I mustn't be very attractive, Beverley was thinking as once again she set off for the glasshouses.

When she was half way there she decided to rest her weary arms and laid down the pot on a garden seat. She sat down beside it and looked about her. The grounds were truly beautifully kept, part of them in formal gardens, while elsewhere nature had been allowed to take its course

with coppices of rowan and birch. How lovely it would be
to live at Kinneil Castle surrounded by these exquisite
grounds! To be free to come and go exactly as one wished!
To buy beautiful and expensive clothes! To drive an expensive sports car!

All the same, in spite of all the luxury of her background,
Lynne didn't seem a truly happy girl. There was something
missing in her life, something which she obviously desired
but did not possess, and for a moment Beverley wondered
if Alex was the one man whom Lynne found unattainable.

But it was time she was returning Tam's precious azalea.

She stood up and grasped the pot, but to her dismay it
slipped from between her fingers and she gave a little
scream of pain as it crashed down on to her foot. The pot
had shattered into fragments and the azalea lay spilled on
the path. She sat down again on the garden seat until the
pain abated, then slowly she began to walk back to the
house, limping slightly.

'What on earth is the matter?' Lynne stood in the doorway.

'Oh, nothing. I've bruised my foot a little,' Beverley told
her hurriedly.

'Dear me, what a pity! Just when I was going to suggest
we look around the gardens and decide on the best places
for the lanterns! I must say you do look as if you'd been in
the wars.' Lynne continued surveying Beverley's dress, now
earth-stained and with a slight tear where the edge of the
pot had caught the frail material.

The words were spoken sympathetically, but as Lynne
turned her head Beverley caught a gleam of satisfaction in
those brilliant green eyes and it dawned on her that the
trips to and from the glasshouses had been no more than
part of a charade set up by Lynne. She tightened her lips.
'Of course I'll be able to help you!' she said quickly. Not for
a moment would she have Lynne know that wandering
about the grounds was the last thing she wanted to do.

Afterwards when they returned to the Castle, Lynne proposed she should drive Beverley back to the Guesthouse, but Beverley shook her head. 'No, thanks, I'll manage!'

And she did too! Although by the time she reached the MacCrimmons' house she was still limping slightly. As she hesitated in the hall she heard the deep tones of Alex's voice in the parlour and decided she would go on upstairs.

But as she put her foot on the first step the parlour door opened and Isa appeared. 'Ah, there you are! I thought I heard someone in the hall. Come away in now. We're having smokies and mustard sauce this evening. I know you enjoy them.'

Beverley shook her head frantically, but Isa refused to give up. 'Now don't be stiffnecked,' she protested. 'You needn't speak to Alex if you don't want to. But you simply must sample the smokies. They're a real treat, straight from Arbroath.'

She was so insistent that reluctantly Beverley followed her into the room. As usual a cosy fire glowed in the grate and the table groaned with food. Morag following them into the room with a tray in her hand beamed at Beverley, but as far as Alex was concerned, she might have been the invisible woman.

'I'm sure this is very different from the food at the Castle,' Morag was saying as she put plates on the table. 'It's Cordon Bleu cooking there, I'm told.'

There was nothing for Beverley to do but to take her place at the table. As she did so, Alex asked, 'What has happened to your foot? It seems to me you've a bit of a limp.'

Nothing escaped Alex's observant eye, she thought crossly.

'Don't tell me you walked back from the Castle!' he continued.

'Of course I did,' she replied tightly. 'It's not a long walk, you know.'

Aware that Alex's perceptive hazel eyes were fixed on her thoughtfully, Beverley launched into a rather feverish discussion of the beauties of the Castle.

'What exactly do you do for Lynne?' Morag enquired curiously.

And when Beverley had begun a recital of her various duties for the day the sisters glanced across at each other knowingly.

'If you ask me it seems you've had more than enough to do today,' Morag said dryly.

'Yes, it's just like Lynne!' put in Isa. 'They do say in the village that she can be very demanding at times.'

Beverley felt herself flush. Did it sound as though she was whining about the work she had to tackle? She flashed a glance in Alex's direction, only to find that his eyes were fixed on her again.

'You haven't told us how you came to hurt your foot,' he remarked.

Instantly Beverley felt her mood change. How dared Alex question her in that abrupt manner, as if he had a right to explanations! Well, she wasn't going to answer up like a good little child, not after his unforgivable behaviour to her!

When she did not reply, but continued eating her Arbroath smokie in a marked silence, Isa coughed nervously. 'And your lovely dress—quite ruined! Did that happen at the same time as you hurt your foot?'

'Oh, it's nothing really,' Beverley said lightly. 'Just a slight tear. It can easily be mended. You see, I was carrying an azalea back to the glasshouses when it slipped from my fingers and—well, I suppose some of the earth spilled on my dress.'

'It must have been a mighty big pot to have injured your foot in that fashion,' Alex said dryly.

She glared at him. 'Yes,' she said loudly, 'as it happens it was enormous and weighed about a ton—now are you satisfied?'

'Really, what is all the excitement about?' he demanded. 'I merely remarked that it must have been rather a large pot.'

'You were being sarcastic, as usual,' retorted Beverley, 'as though I were making a mountain out of a molehill!' To her dismay she could hear her own voice rising shrilly.

Morag glanced about the table, an artificial smile set on her face. 'I think we're all finished now, aren't we? Come, Isa, we'll do up the dishes.'

In a subdued silence the two sisters began to clear the table.

'I'll help you,' Beverley offered.

'Don't dream of moving,' Morag said quickly. 'Sit in an armchair by the fire and take things quietly. You look completely worn out.'

To Beverley's dismay the two sisters disappeared through the door with alacrity, leaving her alone with Alex.

Slowly and carefully Beverley got to her feet and walking as smoothly as possible moved over to an armchair by the fire. She picked up a magazine and began to peruse it, but soon saw, as she risked a quick glance out of the side of her eye, that Alex had apparently no intention of departing.

He strolled across the room, took an armchair opposite her and hitched it closer to the fire. Then slowly and with an air of abstraction he began to fill his pipe.

Her eyes fixed on the printed page, Beverley was secretly fuming. How she would have loved to march across the room and sweep through the door! In the circumstances, of course, this manoeuvre might not be completely successful.

His pipe filled, Alex lit it, and leaned back in his chair surveying the ceiling and puffing contentedly. For some minutes there was silence in the room except for the soft fall of ash in the glowing fire.

She was still staring at the printed page when she heard him say mildly, 'It seems to me you must be a slow reader.'

Beverley put down the magazine. 'Now what do you mean by that?' she snapped, and instantly regretted she had risen to the bait.

'You appear to take rather a long time to read a few columns of print!'

'I can't see what business it is of yours,' she retorted.

'No, perhaps not,' he admitted. 'And now I'm going to risk another question. Would you like me to take a look at your foot?'

'No, I certainly shouldn't,' she told him.

'Pity, because I'm rather good at that sort of thing.'

'I didn't know you'd qualified as a doctor,' she told him sarcastically.

For a few moments he puffed in silence and then said, 'No, of course not! But I have experience of treating all sorts of injuries when it comes to wild life. And you'd be amazed how similar human beings can be in lots of ways.'

'So you're a sort of horse-doctor,' she told him with disdain.

To her annoyance he took no offence at this. 'I suppose you could say that! And although I do say it myself I'm a pretty successful horse-doctor—when it comes to treating wild creatures, at any rate.'

'Well, I'm not part of your wild life!' she shot at him, her eyes sparkling with anger.

Slowly he sat upright and laying down his pipe gazed at her intently and gravely. 'You know, at this moment you look amazingly like an infuriated fawn.'

Feeling completely disconcerted, Beverley sought in her mind for a crushing reply, but the best she could think of was, 'I didn't know a fawn could be infuriated.'

'Well no, perhaps you're right,' he agreed. 'All the same you've got widely spaced eyes and long lashes and when you're angry those big eyes of yours look extraordinarily fawn-like.'

She regarded him with flashing eyes. 'Now you're making fun of me!'

'No, indeed! On the contrary, I——'

But whatever he had been about to say was lost for ever because at that moment the door opened and in came Morag with a pair of carpet slippers in her hand. 'Just the very thing you need,' she announced. 'Now don't you think, all things considered, you ought to have an early night?'

As she was about to help Beverley to put them on, Alex took them from her hand. 'I'm sure, Morag, Isa would like your help in the kitchen,' he told her smoothly.

For a second Morag looked startled, then, to Beverley's fury, she gave them a knowing smile before leaving the room and shutting the door firmly behind her.

Gently Alex eased Beverley's injured foot out of her shoe and put on the carpet slipper.

As he did so she looked up at him with hostile eyes, but he seemed impervious to her reaction. 'I think Morag is right. An early night is what you need.'

'Thanks, but I'm not interested in what you think!' she snapped.

While she was still speaking he lifted her into his arms in a sweeping movement and carried her from the room.

The unexpectedness of the manoeuvre took her so completely by surprise that he was actually climbing the stairs before she got her breath back. 'Will you kindly put me down,' she instructed icily. 'I'm perfectly capable of walking upstairs without your assistance.'

Without answering, he pushed her door open with his foot and dumped her down on her bed. 'I'm going to the Castle early tomorrow morning,' he told her. 'I suggest I drive you there—that is if you insist on going to work tomorrow!'

'And I suggest you do nothing of the kind!' she blazed at him through clenched teeth.

Without answering he turned and strode from the room.

How typical of the man's arrogance, she fumed, as she heard the parlour door shut behind him and silence settle over the house. She eased herself up on one elbow and took a long look at herself in the mirror of her dressing-table. Yes, she did have widely spaced eyes and long lashes. But did that mean she looked fawn-like? Impossible to tell whether Alex had intended his remark as a compliment or whether it had held a covert sneer. Angrily she turned her head away.

But his words lingered in her mind like a puzzle and she wished Morag had not chosen that particular moment to appear on the scene with a pair of carpet slippers.

CHAPTER ELEVEN

ON the following morning Beverley awoke early, but she did not get up at once. If Alex was going to the Castle then she would give him plenty of time to set off on his own. She had no intention of accompanying him. She thrust her foot out from under the bedclothes and gently stretched it. Yes, it was greatly improved. She would be perfectly all right for the walk to the Castle later. It was a beautiful morning, and no doubt the exercise would limber up her foot.

Isa brought her breakfast, and when she had eaten it, she got up and began to dress slowly, keeping an ear cocked for the sound of Alex's departure. By the time she was ready she decided that somehow or other he must have slipped out quietly without her noticing, so she went downstairs, but no sooner had she arrived in the hall than the door of the parlour opened and Alex's huge figure loomed in the threshold.

'I can give you a lift this morning, that is if you don't mind riding in a van,' he told her.

'No, thanks,' she replied sharply. 'It's a beautiful morning. I intend to walk.'

'I don't really think that would be a good idea,' he told her.

'And I really don't much care what you think,' she retorted as she moved across the hall and went out through the door.

But as she hurried along the path she could hear his long strides behind her. There was something ominous about them that made her hurry even faster. She had reached the gate and was about to turn off along the coast road when she found herself swung up in his arms and deposited in the passenger seat of a van which stood outside on the road. In a moment he had slid behind the wheel and the van moved off.

She sat beside him stiffly in silence, then as curiosity overcame her as to why he was driving a van to the Castle, she glanced at him cautiously. But he stared grimly ahead and she decided to say nothing—at least for the time being.

They had hardly stopped before the Castle door before Lynne appeared. 'What happened to you yesterday, Alex?' she began. 'You left no message for me! Why?' Her tone was imperious.

'No, I'm afraid I was very busy yesterday,' he replied coolly, as he put his hand under Beverley's elbow and helped her into the house.

Lynne laughed shortly. 'How gallant you are!' she exclaimed acidly. 'I really don't know why I put up with you, Alex! And how is your foot, Beverley?' her voice was suddenly over-sweet. 'There was no need for you to turn up today, you know.'

'Oh, it's nothing!' Beverley replied quickly. 'It was my own fault. Anyway, I wanted to get on with the drapes. If they're not tackled now they won't be ready on time.'

Lynne nodded. 'That's true. And once you're in the sewing-room you can stay put. You needn't move an inch. I'll have lunch served to you there on a tray. By the way, Alex, what's the idea of the tatty little grey van? Have you gone into the haulage business, or what?'

'Well, yes, you might say I'm a carrier in a small way of business,' he agreed. 'In fact, I've come for the furniture you promised me for the black house and which so far has not materialised.'

'Really, Alex!' Lynne gave a trill of sharp laughter. 'How can I remember a thing like that when I've so much to think of at the moment? Anyway, what on earth has come over you? Why should you bother about armchairs, and china, and such like? It's simply not your scene, is it? I mean, surely you're not *serious*? I suppose you've made up your mind to hold me to my word? Is that it?' she demanded, obviously annoyed.

'You'd be amazed at the way Beverley has civilised me,' he told her easily. 'I'm all for creature comforts now. I've a list somewhere here. Now let's see!' He consulted a slip of paper. 'I need one presentable table in good condition, unscratched, if possible. One armchair, comfortable if possible ditto. Various pieces of china, bone if you have it, but not necessarily matching. We like the best but are not too particular about the pattern. Originality is what we aim for. Now let me see—armchair——'

Lynne gave one of her trilling laughs. 'We? Don't you sound cosy? Don't tell me you're setting up house again with Beverley as your faithful handmaiden?'

Listening to this, Beverley found her blood slowly coming to the boil. She swung round and faced them, her hands clenched. 'I don't know what Alex wants the furniture for,' she told Lynne. 'But far from being cosy, I've no intention of returning again. This has nothing whatsoever to do with me.'

'Dear me, aren't we spirited!' Lynne cooed. 'Who would have thought little Beverley would show such fire!'

Before Beverley could reply Alex's voice said smoothly, 'Perhaps I should have made it plain from the start that I want these little comforts for my wildcats, Punch and Judy, and myself. We're getting along very nicely, I find.'

'Hardly the conventional family!' Lynne said rather acidly.

He considered this thoughtfully. 'No, come to think of it, we could do with some feminine assistance. Will you come back with me to Solan and let me have your valuable advice in setting things in order?'

Beverley could feel herself redden with mortification. She had been foolish enough to think he had been collecting the furniture in an effort to placate her, hoping that perhaps if the house were refurnished she might consider returning to his employment. What he had really been interested in, she now saw, was using the collecting of the furniture as an excuse for inviting Lynne to accompany him to Solan.

And now Lynne was all radiant good-humour. 'First we must get you settled, Beverley,' she said, smiling. 'Then we can have the odds and ends carried down from the attics. There'll be no need for us to consult you, because if you're not returning to Solan, it won't matter to you what they're like. You won't mind if my taste is quite quite different from yours?'

'Not in the least,' Beverley told her tightly. She tried to smile brightly, but knew that her annoyance showed and was glad that Alex had gone out to the van. Quickly she walked across the hall and began to climb the stairs, aware as she did so that she still had a slight limp in her bruised foot, and rather dreading the many flights of stairs that would have to be climbed before she reached her eyrie in the sewing-room.

But at that moment Alex returned. He watched her progress for a moment or two, then to her amazement crossed the hall and once more she was whisked off her feet.

'Put me down!' she cried furiously.

He paid no attention, but went up swiftly, as if she weighed no more than a child.

Enraged at having been treated in this way in front of Lynne, Beverley began to kick him furiously with her heels.

'Wildcats have nothing on you,' he told her coolly. 'And to think I regarded you as a nice, well-brought-up, well-behaved, refined, genteel young lady when you first arrived! It just goes to show you how one can be deceived!' he ended with one of those rare smiles that transformed his face.

He placed her in the chair before the sewing-machine, and afterwards she wondered if he had really kissed her. It had been so light and quick. Had it really happened! She touched her cheek with her fingertip. The kiss had been so fleeting that it was easy to believe she had only imagined it. She pushed the thought away from her as she set to work on the huge pile of material that still remained from the previous day.

As the morning passed she found the work incredibly monotonous. Mile after mile of the pale oyster and yellow striped material seemed to stream under the hammer of the sewing-machine, yet the task was no nearer completion.

Apart from that, she found it hard to concentrate. Only too clearly could she visualise Alex and Lynne in the black house, Lynne, vivacious and witty, while she directed the placing of the different pieces. What would they talk about? They had friends and acquaintances from former years, long before she herself had appeared on the scene. There were parts of their lives closed to her and which she could never share.

As the days passed Beverley discovered that this job at the Castle was turning out quite differently from the way she had imagined it. What had drawn her to it in the first place had been Lynne's promise that it would have an artistic interest. But this was just the part of the work which Lynne kept in her own hands. It was she who made the decisions regarding flower arrangements and colour schemes. In the end Beverley found that even her suggestions concerning the placing of the lanterns had been over-ridden quietly but decisively. All that Beverley had to do was to see that everything was carried out in accordance with Lynne's instructions.

Apart from that, her days were so filled with activity that in the evenings she returned to the Guesthouse feeling completely exhausted. Not only had she to do the sewing of the drapes but she had to help in hanging them, a job she found rather frightening when she had to balance on the very top step of the ladder.

Lynne had hinted at a certain companionship between them, a sharing of the work, but as it turned out Beverley's life was pretty lonely. She found herself in a small, dark room, deep in the depths of the Castle, washing the price-less china which Lynne's mother valued so highly. It was a singularly depressing place, slated and damp and with a view of dank shrubbery. Here there was nothing to distract her thoughts except the sound of water running from a tap into an enormous wooden trough.

Lynne, on the other hand, spent much of her time call-ing up her friends in London, and other distant places. The phone bills must be enormous, Beverley surmised, but then the Redferns were rich, she reminded herself.

The phone calls quickly brought to her side a horde of bright young men and women, and after their arrival Lynne was even more inclined to break up the monotony of the day with riding and swimming. Often as Beverley was carefully lifting the china pieces from the sudsy water, she would see from behind the misted windows Lynne setting off at a canter on her gleaming silken-coated horse. There was a strange streak of loneliness in Lynne which made her often set out by herself, but sometimes her companion on these rides would be a certain Ian Laird who, only too clearly, cared deeply for his capricious young hostess. It was also clear that all the affection was on his side while all that Lynne seemed to feel for him was a casual friendship.

Grudgingly Beverley had to admit to herself that Lynne was a fearless rider, and with a sinking heart she began to see what it was that drew Alex to this tall slim girl with the strange green jewel-like eyes.

It was from the window of this little dark room that she saw Alex drive up one afternoon. For once, the Castle was empty of Lynne's young friends. Those who had been present during the previous few days had gone off on the car-ferry. Beverley knew too that Lynne had set off for a drive in her sports car, so she was not too surprised when a short time later Alex made his appearance.

'I was told you were here,' he told her, leaning against the high cupboard that stood in one corner of the small room.

'Yes, Lynne has gone off for a drive,' she replied dryly. She did not add, otherwise you wouldn't have troubled to give me your company!

With a little start she realised that jealousy consumed her and she felt surprised and put out at her own reaction. After all, she had nothing but dislike for Alex, she told herself. His arrogance was completely unendurable and his rudeness unforgivable. Yet when he chose he could show such tenderness. She felt suddenly confused. If only she could take up an attitude towards him, and maintain it, instead of being swayed by his moods.

His eyes were surveying the dungeon-like room with its floor of slate, a relic of bygone days. 'I can't say this is much of an improvement on the black house,' he remarked dryly. 'Even at its worst, it wasn't as bad as this.'

Instantly Beverley felt her hackles rise. 'No one asked you to come slumming!' she retorted tartly. 'And as far as the black house is concerned, here at least I don't have to put up with your vile manners!'

'I see, so I'm even worse than Lynne, is that it? They tell me she can be quite a tartar when the humour strikes her. A Latin temperament, in spite of the fact that she's a thoroughly English girl!'

'And no doubt you admire a Latin temperament!' she retorted, and instantly regretted the words.

'I don't think you have the slightest conception of what I admire or don't admire,' he replied easily. As he spoke, he took up a cloth and gingerly began to dry one of the plates which had been resting in the wooden rack by the side of the trough.

Aware that she had put herself at a disadvantage, Beverley swung round. 'Put that down!' she snapped. 'I'm responsible for this china. If anything happens to it, *I'm* the one who'll get the blame.'

Alex tossed the cloth aside. 'Just as you say! Actually this is not my scene. I'd be a little awkward, not having been trained for it, you might say.'

'It seems to me,' she told him, 'that you've plenty of time on your hands recently. When I was at the black house you never had a moment to spare.'

'Ah, that's because I've now become a gentleman of leisure,' he told her with satisfaction. 'My paper on the kits is finished and I'm taking a short pause before plunging back into work.'

'I see,' she said flatly. So that was why he was such a frequent visitor to the Castle! Now that he had some time to spare he was spending his leisure with Lynne.

Just then, through the barred windows they glimpsed Lynne's sports car flash along the drive and swing to a stop in Lynne's usual dashing style on the wide gravel apron before the Castle. To Beverley's surprise, when Lynne had slipped from behind the wheel, a small girl with long dark hair scrambled out after her.

'So Mandy has arrived!' remarked Alex, his eyes on the child, who seemed to be hanging back sulkily, so that Lynne had to catch her by the hand and almost pull her indoors.

'Mandy?' Beverley looked at him enquiringly.

'She's Lynne's young cousin. Lynne takes her on occasionally when her aunt Evelyn wants a free hand for a few days. Repayment for past favours, in fact. It seems her aunt has often stood between Lynne and her parents when she's got herself into scrapes. Otherwise I don't see Lynne taking on a child as extraordinary as Mandy. She can set the household on its ear when she's in the mood for it.'

'Spoken like a typical bachelor!' Beverley remarked. 'I feel sure she's not half as bad as you make her out. But then I don't suppose you care for children in any shape or form.'

'On the contrary, I'm devoted to children,' he replied to her annoyance, 'especially small chubby ones under a year old.'

'Just the age when you would have nothing to do with them!' she told him as she placed a dripping sauce-boat on the rack. 'It would be a different thing later on when they might obtrude on your routine.'

'Don't tell me you two are fighting!' Lynne had appeared in the doorway. 'Or are you simply chatting her up, Alex? One can never tell, with you!'

'I did think my presence might brighten this rather gloomy spot,' he replied, to Beverley's surprise. 'It looks as if it might have been a dungeon in days gone by.'

Lynne bit her lip, then flashed him one of her artificial smiles. 'Nonsense! We have no dungeons here. If there ever were any they've been filled in ages ago. Now hadn't you better leave Beverley to get on with the job? You can be rather distracting at times, you know. But then no one knows that better than Beverley, I'm sure,' she added with a sharp glance in Beverley's direction.

'I've just finished,' Beverley assured her, trying to hide her annoyance. 'And no accidents either!' she added.

'Good!' Lynne replied. 'In that case don't let's just stand here. I've ordered tea. I suggest we take a break and have a cuppa.' She flashed Beverley a bright including smile, and Beverley dried her hands in a towel and accompanied them up the stone stairs to the hall.

'And where's the demon child?' asked Alex as Lynne presided behind the tea things.

'Oh, I sent her down to Cook,' Lynne replied. 'She's even more of a handful this time, I've discovered. She hates the idea of her mother going off to Paris and leaving her behind. I must say I do wish she hadn't chosen this particular time for a second honeymoon, just when we're getting ready for the ball.'

'Yes, I suppose it's awkward for you,' Alex said slowly. 'But then I suppose no matter when Mandy arrived, it would be an awkward time for you.'

'Yes, and I simply must go to Edinburgh tomorrow,' Lynne agreed. 'It's a good thing you're here, Beverley. You'll be able to keep an eye on her! The idea of letting that dreadful child rove about on her own all day is quite out of the question. All that would happen would be that we should lose a perfectly good cook.'

'I see,' Alex said thoughtfully. 'Yes, it's convenient, Beverley being here. All the same, don't you think you're letting her in for a pretty hectic day?'

The reprimand in his voice was unmistakable and Lynne's eyes glinted as she replied sweetly, 'How charming of you to be so protective, Alex! I'm sure Beverley's capable of fighting her own corner, aren't you, Beverley dear?'

Beverley who had been listening to this conversation with rising indignation replied quickly, 'I'm quite used to children. I have a sister much younger than myself.'

'Have you indeed!' Alex interjected. 'But then I suppose

she's an ordinary conventional sort of child. No one, not even the least observant, could take Mandy for an ordinary child!'

'All the same, I'm perfectly capable of taking care of her for a day! I'm not utterly useless,' Beverley told him sharply.

'Yes, and I shan't impose on her—if that's what you're hinting!' Lynne went on. 'All I'm asking Beverley to do is to take the child down to the beach—the cove with the white sands would be ideal. It's almost enclosed and there would be very little chance of Mandy getting up to mischief there. I'll have Cook make up a basket of goodies,' she told Beverley. 'You can spend the day there and have a picnic. It will be a nice change from washing the china. At least you'll be able to have a day in the fresh air.'

So Lynne already had it all organised, Beverley was thinking with annoyance. She had not even been consulted. In spite of that, she knew she was rather looking forward to the following day. It would be nice to spend the day by the sea, while Lynne was safely in Edinburgh. She would make sure the child was properly occupied! Probably if the child was mischievous it was because she was bored.

'Oh, by the way,' Alex said as he got to his feet, 'it seems that the MacCrimmons are not going to be among those present on the great night.'

'What do you mean?' Lynne asked.

'Just before I left they received word that a relative of theirs is very ill on the Mainland. They were discussing what they ought to do and as far as I know they've decided they ought to visit him. That would mean they wouldn't be back until your do is over.'

'Dear me, what a pity!' Lynne said with conventional regret. 'You must tell them how disappointed I am.' She paused thoughtfully. 'So there'll be no party from the Guesthouse this year. You'll be arriving on your own, Alex.'

'True,' he agreed. 'I'm sure I shall rather miss the sisters keeping a sharp eye out to see what I get up to!'

On the following morning Beverley arrived to find Lynne already dressed for her trip to Edinburgh. She was wearing a dress and short jacket of fine pale silvery green which somehow seemed to make her hair appear even more fair than usual. She carried a handbag of palest leaf brown leather and wore matching elegant shoes.

'And this is Mandy,' Lynne said, pushing forward a child with lank black hair and sullen dark eyes. 'Shake hands nicely with Beverley,' she told the child sharply.

Mandy glared up at Beverley under an untidy fringe.

The little girl was unusually pale, Beverley noted, and decided that she probably was indoors too much.

'Now I want you to be extra specially good today,' Lynne admonished, 'and go down to the cove with Beverley and have a nice picnic.'

'Mummy said *you* would take care of me,' the child announced bellicosely.

'Not today,' Lynne replied crisply. 'I'm going to Edinburgh. So just do as you're told and don't make a nuisance of yourself.'

She turned to Beverley, pulling on her gloves as she spoke. 'You'll find everything you need for the day in that big cupboard at the end of the passageway: there are deckchairs, and beach umbrellas, and air-mattresses, and whatnot. Be sure to take an air-mattress. Perhaps Mandy might take a nap during the day,' she added hopefully. 'But you will keep a strict eye on her? Aunt Evelyn is so dreadfully fussy, and would never forgive me if I let her get into any mischief. Of course I know you're a very sensible person and very conscientious,' she added condescendingly.

Trust Lynne to make it so very plain that she regards me as stuffy and dull, Beverley was thinking resentfully as Lynne moved swiftly across the hall and disappeared from view. A moment later came the sound of her car door banging and she was gone.

Left alone with the sullen Mandy, Beverley decided that the sooner they got organised and went down to the cove the better. But it took two trips before they settled themselves with everything they needed. From the cupboard Lynne had mentioned Beverley picked out a beach umbrella to shade them from the bright sun which could glance so blindingly from the sea and white sands. She took a folding canvas chair and a bright red air-mattress. After a little thought she included a shrimping net; perhaps she could interest the child in the rocky pools in the two arms of boulders which enclosed the pretty bay.

When eventually everything, including the picnic basket, had been lugged to the cove, Beverley settled herself in the canvas chair under the umbrella while Mandy unenthusiastically pottered on the beach with a little spade and bucket. From her seat Beverley could look straight across to Solan, and she experienced a little wave of nostalgia. How enchanted it looked, she thought. But what a busy life she had lived when she had taken care of the black house! How was it that she was not happier now that she was spending the day in idleness, instead of being at the beck and call of that arrogant taskmaster, Alex Ramage?

But she was not to be left long to her thoughts. Mandy had wandered back towards her and now stood before her looking up with that strange baleful glare.

'Well, did you make a nice sand-castle?' Beverley enquired hopefully.

'Sand-castles are stupid,' announced Mandy flatly.

'Then what about collecting some pretty shells?' Beverley suggested.

'I hate shells,' Mandy told her uncompromisingly.

'Oh! Then what are you going to do?' There was no doubt about it, Mandy was a problem child, Beverley was thinking.

Mandy considered this for a moment, then brightened. 'I know. I'll catch a crab with my net, a great big one, and I'll bring it back in my bucket and I'll let it bite your toes.'

Taking up her bucket and shrimping net, she trudged off sturdily towards one of the lines of rocky pools that edged the little bay.

Seeing that the child seemed engrossed in searching the pools for her giant crab Beverley took a paperback from her pocket and was soon absorbed. Occasionally she glanced up to see that Mandy was getting up to no mischief, but gradually the salty air and the warm sun made her eyes close sleepily. After all, she told herself, she had been working pretty hard for the previous few days. A little nap would be welcome. Just a short one, she assured herself as her eyelids drooped and she dozed off.

Her dream was of a desert island with waving palms and golden sands in which in some vague way Alex was involved, a dream which turned to nightmare as there came to her ears the screams of a child, shrill but far away.

She sat up, suddenly wide awake and with her heart beating uncomfortably. Her first glance was for the rocky pools, and as she saw that there was no longer a small absorbed figure there she felt panic grip her throat. Again there came the sound of a scream, fainter now, and as Beverley's eyes flew to the sea she caught a glimpse of the red air-mattress. Upon it a small figure crouched in terror.

CHAPTER TWELVE

FOR a moment Beverley gazed, petrified with horror. The mattress was bobbing in the rough water that flowed in the channel that divided Solan from Kinneil. How much longer would Mandy be able to cling on?

Beverley pulled off her sandals, splashed wildly through the shallows and when the shore suddenly shelved launched herself into the deeper water, swimming as fast as she could. But soon, as the water grew rougher and the currents stronger, she realised there was no possibility of overtaking that bobbing red mattress before it was swept around the end of Solan. But Mandy was quiet now and Beverley felt sure that the child had seen her and felt reassured that an attempt was being made to save her. There was nothing for it but to keep that bright red speck in sight and keep swimming after it.

How long the situation remained like this Beverley was never afterwards able to tell, but into the dreamlike state that had come over her she heard the put-put of an outboard motor. She raised her head almost indifferently, so tired did she feel and so hopeless. But what she saw instantly restored her. In the dinghy was Alex's unmistakable figure and already he was altering course. The small boat swung around and set off in pursuit of Mandy. Minutes later it was setting off for Solan, Mandy safely inside.

And now Beverley had a curious sense of let-down. Her first delight in the safety of the child was replaced by a realisation of her own plight. She felt sure Mandy had seen her, but was the child too young to be able to let Alex know that she too was in need of assistance. She raised her head, trying to assess her position and realised that she was almost half way between the two islands. But swimming towards Kinneil was much easier than heading into the currents around Solan, so she turned in that direction.

How far away the shore seemed, she thought almost languidly as time passed and she seemed to be making little headway. She could catch a glimpse now and then of the bright beach umbrella, a splash of colour against the white of the sand. What a long time ago it seemed since she had sat there reading her paperback and drowsing in the warmth of the sun.

Then she heard once more the sound of the outboard motor. It was very near now, coming up behind her. She turned her head and found herself looking up into Alex's face.

Next moment she was hauled upwards and found herself lying speechless and exhausted in the bottom of the boat as Alex turned it in the direction of Solan. She ventured a few incoherent words, but he silenced her with a gesture. 'Don't try to speak. Just take things easy.' And glad to obey, she let herself slump into semi-unconsciousness, aware of nothing but the fact that at last she was safe.

It seemed only moments later that she found herself close to a blazing fire of dried bracken and peat. She looked about rather dazedly. So she was in the black house once more! Then she sat up in alarm. 'Mandy!' she exclaimed. 'Where is she?'

Alex pointed across to a big armchair in which the child lay curled up already fast asleep. 'It doesn't take children long to come around from their adventures,' Alex remarked with one of his rare smiles. 'And whatever Mandy's faults, and she has plenty of them, she has lots of courage.'

As Beverley gazed at the sleeping child she felt a little surge of protectiveness. 'She looks so innocent and attractive when she's asleep,' she remarked, 'yet she can be so cheeky when she's awake.'

'I shouldn't blame the child altogether,' Alex told her. 'Her mother pays no attention to her when she's at home, and just dumps her on Lynne when she wants to go off on a jaunt. Lynne, of course, gives Mandy very little of her time, because she's always on the go herself. Anyway, she's not exactly the motherly type,' he added dryly. 'And now, as Mandy's warm and dry and you're certainly not, I suggest you slip out of your clothes and dry them in front of the fire.'

'I shall do nothing of the sort,' Beverley snapped. 'Anyway, why did you bring me here? I was heading for Kinneil. I can't have been far from the shore when you picked me up.'

'Considering the MacCrimmons are getting ready to

visit a relative who's very ill on the Mainland, I felt that bringing in someone half drowned wouldn't be exactly good for their nerves.'

'Oh!' Beverley bit her lip, feeling rather taken aback. It was like Alex to do these unexpected considerate things which seemed to be so much in contrast to his usual blunt uncompromising behaviour.

'That's all very well,' she told him, 'but just where am I to change?'

'Don't worry,' he replied gravely. 'I have it all organised. I shall retire to the peat house and stack up some more fuel. Meanwhile you can get into this while your things dry.' As he spoke he reached behind the door and took down a tweed coat which he occasionally wore in bad weather. 'A bit shabby,' he admitted, regarding it critically, 'but genuine Harris tweed. The sort of coat that's handed down from generation to generation—that is if one is keen on that sort of thing,' he ended dryly.

No, Alex was not 'keen on that sort of thing', Beverley was thinking a few minutes later as she shrugged off her wet clothes and draped the voluminous coat about her. It was rather like wearing a tent, she was thinking, as she found that it trailed on the floor behind her in a sort of train. The sleeves were so long that she had to fold them back almost to the shoulders. She shook her wet hair out and tried to fluff it dry in front of the fire. But there was of course no brush or comb. What a spectacle she would present when Alex returned! What a contrast to the exquisitely groomed Lynne Redfern! Still, there was nothing she could do about it, so she shrugged aside the thought and began to look about her.

What changes had come over the black house since she had last seen it! There was now no sign of the kits. Even their boxes had been removed and that part of the house in which animals had formerly been kept was now quite empty. Then there was the fireplace. So Alex had built one after all. He had promised her he would do so one day, but he had waited until after her departure to carry it out. Then there was the furniture that Lynne had supplied! The pieces were old and elegant and looked decidedly incongruous against the smoke-blackened walls.

She went out to the door and beckoned to Alex and as he re-entered with a great bundle of peat in his arms Mandy awoke.

Immediately she sat up and began to examine her surroundings with interest. 'I like it here,' she announced, jumping off the armchair and going to the racks on which Alex kept his specimens. Her head on one side she examined these closely, peering into the jars with great interest.

'And now what about a cup of tea?' Alex asked. 'You look to me like a girl whose appetite has returned.'

It was true, Beverley was thinking, as Alex put a light to the gas and set the kettle to boil. Seated here comfortably before the blazing fire, warm and dry with Alex's old tweed coat wrapped around her, she was already beginning to forget her adventures and rather to enjoy the situation.

'And for something to eat how about a sandwich, a real doorstep one with plenty of meat and chutney? The Mac-Crimmons were so busy this morning that for once I was able to get my own way and make up the sandwiches the way I like them.'

'I'd like that, especially the chutney——'

She stopped, holding her breath, because Mandy was coming across the floor, her step rather unsteady because she was holding up very carefully one of Alex's precious specimen jars. Inside was a particularly hideous beetle.

'May I have him?' she asked anxiously as she reached Alex.

Beverley stiffened, waiting for the storm to break. She was used to Alex's rage if anyone interfered with the specimens. To her surprise, he said nothing, only reached out to take the jar from Mandy's tiny hand. 'Wouldn't you like something rather prettier? A starfish perhaps?' he asked.

Mandy shook her head vigorously. 'No, I like this one. He's ugly and sort of friendly.'

'I see what you mean,' Alex told her gravely. 'All right, you can have it. But be careful it doesn't escape. What would your mother think if she found it walking about the house in the middle of the night!'

'I'll take good care of it,' Mandy assured him. 'I'll keep it in my bedroom, and Mummy won't know he's there, because she hardly ever comes to my bedroom anyway.'

The matter-of-fact tone in which Mandy spoke of her mother's indifference made Beverley warm to the child. 'Come, Mandy, we're going to have tea now,' she said.

And when Mandy had consumed several cups of tea and had tucked into the doorstep sandwiches she curled up in the armchair and once again nodded off.

'As soon as our things are dry we'd better set off for Kinneil,' Beverley remarked. 'We'd better get Mandy home again before Lynne returns from Edinburgh.'

Alex nodded. He replenished the fire, filled his pipe and sat back contentedly. It was a little like playing house, Beverley thought, a little sleepily. A stranger might have mistaken them for father and mother with a sleeping child.

'You look as if you're having pleasant thoughts!'

She glanced at him quickly to find that his strange perceptive eyes were fixed on her. She was glad of the glow of the fire, hoping it would disguise the pink she felt come into her cheeks. 'Oh, I wasn't thinking anything in particular,' she said hastily. 'But it did strike me that you have a way with children. Mandy really likes you.'

'Why shouldn't she?' he asked slowly. 'Perhaps I don't appear such an ogre to her.'

'But that's not really how I see you,' she began a little lamely.

'Come, Beverley, you look upon me as some sort of

misanthrope who hates children, and marriage and domestic ties.'

'Well, now you've said it, yes, that's exactly how I do see you,' she admitted, squaring her chin determinedly.

He fingered his pipe thoughtfully. 'You seem to have all the wrong ideas about me. Actually I do like children—oh, not all of them, I admit. But I like Mandy because she's a fighter. Pretty, prunes-and-prisms little girls don't particularly appeal to me. Actually, if I ever were to have a daughter I'd like her to be exactly like Mandy. Later perhaps a few of her rougher edges might be toned down a little!' he added with a faint smile.

Beverley looked at him in surprise. 'Do you mean you've actually thought about having a daughter, what she'd be like, and all that?'

'Of course! Why the astonishment? I've always looked forward to having a family of my own, something to work for. Do you really think I'm contented out here on Solan with nothing but the wild birds and the animals for company?'

'But I thought you *liked* that sort of life!'

'Yes, of course I like it—but not exactly like this for always! A man must look to the future. For a long time I thought it was just that I'd never met the right girl. Then when I did, I realised it would never work out. My kind of life is too rough and ready.'

He was speaking of Lynne, of course. Beverley turned her head away, suddenly overwhelmed by a cloud of misery and frustration. Was her life from now on to be filled with the thought of what might have been? Of shared moments like these? She dared not look at him in case he should read in her eyes how she longed that she was the one he cared for.

But there was something that must be said before they left the black house for ever. She drew a deep breath and set her features rigidly. 'I want to thank you for rescuing

Mandy and myself,' she told him in a direct clear voice. 'If anything had happened to the child I should never have been able to forgive myself. I should never have been able to remember Solan with happiness. It would have become a place of horror for me. And that's not how I want to think of it, when I go away for ever.'

Alex did not reply and as the silence lengthened she began to wonder if he had even been listening to her.

Then turning his head slowly, he said in a low tone, 'And what about me?'

'What—what do you mean?' She could hear her own voice falter.

'Do you realise, Beverley, that if anything had happened to you I could never have returned to Solan either? Tell me, why do you think I've gone to the trouble of refurnishing the black house? You don't suppose I did it for my own sake? I did it so that when you came back you would see it as you like it to be. But then you can wind me around your little finger, and looking back now I see you've done so ever since you first arrived, looking so very assured, but, I suspect, shaking a little at the knees.'

'I—I wasn't shaking at the knees!' she protested. But she knew she was just talking to disguise the happiness his words gave her. 'Anyway, how could you be so sure I would come back to Solan?'

'That's because I'm smarter than you are,' he told her. 'I knew that the black house would call you back. And now that you're here what are we going to do about the forthcoming ball at the Castle? Do you think we're on sufficiently good terms to go together?'

'Yes, yes, I'd like that,' she said eagerly. How often had she dreamed that in some way or other their differences could be made up, and that, in the end, they would dance together at the Castle. Now it had come about—and in such a strange way! 'But only if you promise to wear that glamorous Highland rig-out,' she told him.

'The kilt, in other words.'

'Yes, complete with all the trimmings!'

'Even to the *skean dhu* in my sock?'

Time flew past as they talked together. Once Alex interrupted what he was saying to put in quickly. 'Don't worry about what Lynne is going to say about all this. She's bound to be annoyed, so I'll take Mandy back and face the music for you.'

And Beverley had not told him then that she had every intention of accepting the blame for Mandy's misadventure. She was not afraid of Lynne, she told herself, although inwardly she quailed at the prospect of what lay ahead.

But she pushed the future into the background of her mind. This moment was all that counted, and this moment she had Alex to herself while Mandy slumbered peacefully before the fire.

She reached out her hand to feel if her dress was dry and he said, 'Somehow I think I'll always remember you as you are now. Yours is an elfin beauty. You don't need a background of beautiful dresses and make-up and hair-do's. You manage to look wonderful wearing an old tweed coat about twenty sizes too big, and as far as I'm concerned that's the test of real beauty.'

He laughed softly, but the sound awoke Mandy, who sat up and rubbed her eyes sleepily.

Their precious time together was over, Beverley knew, and she said, 'Come on, Mandy, we'd better get ready to go back to Kinneil. Lynne will be wondering what's become of you.'

'Must we go back?' Mandy asked sulkily. 'I'd far rather stay here, just you and Alex and me. The Castle's so terribly big. And anyway I think it's haunted.'

'Nonsense!' Beverley said briskly. 'It's beautiful, and any little girl would love to live there.'

'Well, I don't,' Mandy told her uncompromisingly.

This was a return of the old troublesome Mandy, and

Beverley sighed as she got the child ready, for Mandy made everything as difficult as she possibly could. When eventually they were about to set off, Mandy managed to make a diversion over the problem of smuggling her beetle into the Castle, and it was only when Alex had promised to put the jar in his pocket and slip it to her once they were safely inside the Castle that Mandy agreed to make a move homewards.

Then Beverley and Alex nearly quarrelled again when, as the boat touched the shores of Kinneil, she made it plain that she intended to accompany Mandy to the Castle.

'Really, Beverley, you're the most stubborn girl!' he said, annoyed. 'You know you've gone through just as much as you can endure for one day. You should go straight back to the Guesthouse, while I take Mandy home.'

'But I can't do that!' she protested. 'This whole business was my fault. I can't back out now and evade responsibility. You know you wouldn't do anything like that yourself, Alex.'

Reluctantly he gave way, but as they approached the Castle, Beverley felt her heart sink because before the door was Lynne's sports car, and waiting for them in the doorway was Lynne herself.

She rushed forward, her eyes wide, her lipstick gleaming scarlet against pale cheeks, and clasped Mandy in her arms, laughing and crying hysterically.

But when eventually Mandy wriggled out of her grasp and disappeared indoors, Lynne straightened and turned her attention on Beverley. And now there were no more tears. Instead, her eyes blazed with rage. And Beverley got the impression, as she saw Lynne's swift sidewards glance towards Alex, that the emotional scene with the child had been intended to impress him.

'How dare you come here coolly like this!' she cried. 'Do you realise we thought Mandy had been drowned?'

'Beverley too might have been drowned! Did that not

strike you!' Alex put in dryly. 'Come on, Lynne, let's have no more of this. Or at least let's get indoors.'

But once inside the hall of the Castle Lynne returned to the attack. 'It so happened that someone passing on the road saw Mandy drifting out to sea on the air-mattress, and brought the news here. They phoned me in Edinburgh. Can you imagine how I felt? I was utterly devastated!' She swung on Beverley. 'And to think I trusted you! And now you coolly walk in here without a word of explanation!'

'You're hardly giving her time to give an explanation, are you?' Alex remarked. 'But here goes! It chanced that as I was returning to Kinneil I spotted Mandy floating out to sea on the mattress. I managed to get her off in one piece and brought her back to the black house, and that would have been the end of the matter. But Mandy's a smart child. She was able to tell me that Beverley was swimming out after her. So I took the boat out again and by good luck was able to spot her—just in time—and bring her in too.'

'I see! So you brought them both back to the black house. Why didn't you bring them here, or even to the Guesthouse?' Lynne was regarding them with narrowed eyes.

'Remember, you were in Edinburgh,' Alex said patiently. 'And the MacCrimmons have enough on their plates at the moment. All in all the black house seemed the best place to go, somewhere in which we could dry off, and recover at our leisure.'

'So very cosy!' Lynne said acidly. 'But all this is getting us away from the fact that Beverley didn't keep an eye on Mandy as she promised. What were you doing, Beverley, that Mandy was able to float out to sea without your even noticing?'

'I—I thought Mandy was looking for crabs in the rock pools,' Beverley admitted guiltily. 'And I—well, I dozed off for a little while. It was so warm there in the cove and——'

But Lynne didn't let her finish. 'You dozed off! Really, you have a nerve to admit it! What would I have said to her mother if any harm had befallen Mandy? On top of that, instead of coming straight back here you spend your time at the black house, gossiping over tea and muffins, I suppose, while everyone here is distracted with worry, and I'm out of my wits in Edinburgh, not knowing what has happened to the child!'

'Not tea and muffins!' Alex assured her, his voice grim. 'We believe in the simple life on Solan. But don't you think this has gone far enough, Lynne? Beverley has admitted that the whole thing was her fault. And she did try to save the child's life! She could easily have been drowned herself—you know what the currents are like around here. And Beverley's not a particularly good swimmer.'

'I see! How noble of her!' Lynne sneered.

Beverley could see that Alex's defence of her was only increasing Lynne's rage.

'Just what do you expect, Alex?' Lynne demanded. 'Congratulate her on neglecting her duties and——'

'Cut it out!' Alex's voice broke in brusquely. 'The kid's back, so do shut up!'

For a long moment Lynne was silent as though stunned by his remark. Then once again her eyes narrowed and she glanced from one to the other with a strange expression that Beverley found impossible to interpret.

'I see!' And now her voice was completely altered, low and apologetic in tone. 'I'm afraid I did rather fly off the handle. After all, all's well that end's well.'

'Exactly!' Alex agreed a little grimly. 'And now, Beverley, perhaps we'd better be getting back to the Guesthouse.'

'You'll have a drink before you go,' Lynne said quickly. It was clear that she was anxious to placate Alex.

But he answered, 'Thanks, no. I'm afraid we'll have to be getting back right away. With luck we'll be in before the sisters hear anything of today's adventures.'

'Oh, very well, just as you wish!' Lynne accepted defeat. She turned to Beverley. 'I'm sorry for losing my rag in that way. I hope nothing I've said will prevent you coming here tomorrow as usual.'

Beverley hesitated and Alex put in quickly, 'I'm afraid that's impossible. The MacCrimmons want her to take care of the Guesthouse while they're away. There'll be people applying for accommodation at this time and, all in all, it will have to be kept in order until they return.'

Lynne smiled tightly. 'Well, it will be a change for you and Beverley to be out from under the sisters' watchful eyes for a little while.'

A silence followed this and Beverley was aware of Mandy standing watchfully in the background. So the child was waiting patiently until Alex should have the chance of slipping her the precious jar containing the beetle. Beverley fully expected Lynne to catch sight of her at any moment and order her off to bed. But as they went out Lynne remained by the fire and Mandy ran after them. In a moment Alex had transferred the jar into her eager hands and with a breathless word of thanks she had disappeared around the side of the house.

'To think I was at my wits' end to know how to interest that child this morning!' Beverley remarked as they set off. 'If only I'd known that a truly repulsive beetle was all I needed.'

Later, as they drew near the Guesthouse, she asked, 'What do you think Lynne will do if she finds out about Mandy's beetle? Will she let her keep it?'

'Who knows?' Alex replied. 'Lynne is a very complex person. I've always found it difficult to know how her mind works.'

She stole a glance at him, but was unable to read his expression. Perhaps it was Lynne's complex character that held the key to her attraction for him!

CHAPTER THIRTEEN

On the following morning the sisters were up even earlier than usual. It was seldom they left Kinneil and it was easy to see that in spite of their anxiety for their relation they were deriving a certain amount of excitement out of this departure from their usual routine.

But when at last all was ready and Alex and Isa had got into the car, Morag lingered behind with some last minute instructions for Beverley.

'I've left a list of our usual guests, so if any of them get in touch with you, you can safely take bookings. But if anyone else should come along—well, in that case I leave it to your discretion, and——'

But at that moment Isa's voice called that if she delayed any longer they would miss the boat.

'Coming,' Morag called. She lowered her voice. 'Oh, just one other thing. For the past few mornings Alex has been taking pease brose for breakfast. I don't know why, but he's suddenly got a taste for it.'

'Pease brose?' Beverley repeated, completely at sea.

'Yes, it's dried peas ground down to a powder, like a sort of flour. You'll find it in the brown jar on the dresser. All you do is mix it with water until it's a paste then cook it and add a pat of butter and a dash of salt. Mind you,' Morag added disapprovingly, 'some take it with syrup. But Alex likes his with salt in the good old Highland way.'

'I'll try to remember,' Beverley promised, feeling rather dazed by this addition to all the instructions she had received.

'I should hope so,' Morag said rather sternly, 'because if a man doesn't get a really nourishing breakfast in the morning then you'll have a bad-tempered bear of a man on your hands.'

Beverley found it hard to suppress a smile at Morag's earnest manner. 'I'm used to Alex's bearish ways,' she said. 'All the same, I'll try to supply him with his favourite breakfast.'

'Pease brose is what made the Highlanders the fine big hefty folk they are,' Morag assured Beverley, as she hurried out to the car.

To Beverley's relief, she found it quite easy to cope with housekeeping at the Guesthouse. Her cooking was, of course, not up to Morag's standard, but Alex seemed quite satisfied with the dishes she placed before him, when he returned from Solan for his evening meal. To her secret relief he didn't even tease her when she experimented with a difficult dish and produced a near-disaster.

After breakfast each morning, when Alex had gone off to Solan, she took a special pleasure in cleaning and polishing until the whole house sparkled, so that, even if the sisters were to return without warning, they would be pleasantly surprised.

There were some applications from the list of 'regulars' that the sisters had left behind. But one morning as Beverley was carrying out the breakfast dishes she saw an expensive car drive up and a well-dressed couple come walking along the short path to the house. When they rang the bell, she went out and found that they were looking for accommodation for that night.

Beverley hesitated. The name they gave was not on the MacCrimmons' list, but she did not like to refuse the application of such an obviously well-heeled couple.

The woman was dressed in a beautifully cut suit, her white hair drawn back into a chignon, her features rather horsily aristocratic. Her husband too, a short stout man with a bristling moustache, was dressed in clothes that were impeccably tailored.

'I'm told,' he barked, 'that there's no decent hotel on this island.'

'That's true,' Beverley agreed. 'In fact there's no hotel. But then Kinneil isn't very big and most of the summer visitors are taken in by the local people.'

'That's all very well,' the woman interjected, 'but I'm afraid that sort of thing wouldn't do for us at all. We've been told that the MacCrimmon guesthouse is the best possible place to look for accommodation. You're one of the Miss MacCrimmons, possibly?'

'No, the sisters are not here at the moment,' Beverley told her.

'Then who are you?' the woman demanded.

'I'm just a guest here,' Beverley told her.

The woman glanced at her husband with a raised eyebrow of exasperation.

'But this is very awkward,' she told Beverley. 'My husband is interested in a hunting ground that's to rent for the autumn, and has come to inspect it, but as it seems there's no proper hotel—I think, if we'd known of this in time, we would have hesitated about coming. However, it seems the MacCrimmons have quite a good name for plain comfortable accommodation. All the same, we'd like to have a look around before deciding.'

As she spoke she moved forward as if bent on entering the hall, but Beverley did not stand aside. Was this the sort of people the sisters would wish to have as their guests? she was asking herself. At the same time she would dearly have loved to accept their booking. It would have been nice to be able to show the sisters how efficiently she had managed during their absence.

'Come, girl, are you or are you not going to let us in?' barked the stout man.

'No, I don't think we are,' said Alex's voice.

Beverley could feel his tall strength behind her, and she found it strangely comforting. The couple raised their eyes to encounter Alex's gaze and it was plain they felt disconcerted by the presence of this man who so obviously knew his own mind.

As they stared at him in blank amazement Beverley could scarcely restrain a giggle.

'What—what did you say?' the man asked.

'I suggest you look for accommodation elsewhere,' Alex told him.

'But why?' the woman demanded. 'Don't tell me the guesthouse is full—not at this time of the year!'

'That's true,' Alex agreed. 'Nevertheless we can't accept you as guests.'

When, after a few moments more of bluster, the couple turned and walked back towards their car, Alex said with satisfaction, 'Well, that disposes of them!' He took Beverley's arm and led her indoors. 'I can't imagine what you were dithering about anyway. They seemed a singularly unpleasant couple—not the type the MacCrimmons usually have here.'

'All the same,' Beverley demurred as they went into the parlour, 'I'd have liked to show the sisters that I'd snared a couple of lucrative customers.'

'Don't be so sure the booking would have been lucrative,' he told her. 'Often, the better-off people are, the meaner they are!'

'Now you're being cynical,' she said crossly as she folded the tablecloth. 'Anyway, you were every bit as rude as they were.'

'Was I?' He appeared surprised. 'I thought I was the soul of courtesy.'

'That's because it's natural for you to be dictatorial and imperious towards people,' she told him severely. 'It seems to me that a few lessons in courtesy wouldn't do you any harm.'

Once again she heard his deep laugh. 'Somehow I can't see myself bowing from the waist and kissing a lady's hand.'

'You know perfectly well I don't mean that! I'm speaking of ordinary common or garden politeness.'

Beverley placed the tablecloth in the sideboard drawer, as she had seen the sisters do, and Alex said quietly, 'I want you to come here and sit down in this chair for a while.'

She turned and looked at him and something in his glance made her heart beat faster as she took her place opposite him.

He gazed into the fire for a moment or two and then said, 'Hasn't it occurred to you that I might have other reasons for rejecting visitors?'

'No,' she said slowly, wondering what he was about to say.

'Then I'd better tell you that the real reason I wouldn't accept those two was that I don't want anyone breaking in upon our lives here. I don't know if you've realised it, but it seems to me that at last you and I are getting on well together, and I don't want the spell to be broken by nosy intruders.'

As her first rush of delight ebbed some little devil of mischief made her say, 'But why? Lots of girls are better housekeepers than I am, and I think you'll admit I'm not the world's best cook!'

'I don't give a dash what your cooking is like,' he protested with some of his old brusqueness. 'I agree with you, of course, that there are plenty of girls who are better housekeepers. But they wouldn't be you! You see, I like things as they are, and I want to keep them that way as long as possible.'

And Beverley felt a warm glow at her heart as she realised that Alex too wanted these idyllic days to continue.

Other men had paid her compliments and she had taken them on their surface value, but from Alex words like these were like priceless jewels to be stowed away and taken out like secret treasures from time to time.

She had been rather dreading that the sisters might

return unexpectedly and break the web of enchantment that hung over their lives, and it was with a sense of relief that she received a postcard saying that although their relative was on the mend they would stay on for a day or two longer on the Mainland. Typically, Morag had added a postscript. 'Hope you have mastered the pease brose.'

Laughingly, Beverley read it out to Alex.

'You haven't, you know,' he told her.

'Haven't what?'

'Mastered the pease brose! It's still lumpy and you don't put in half enough salt. But then how could I expect it, when you yourself take sugar with your porridge.'

'And why not?' she demanded unrepentantly. 'I can't imagine how you Scots endure it with salt.'

'Then you'll never be a true Scotswoman,' he assured her.

'No, I suppose not!' she agreed, thinking how strange it was that even a light remark like this intended as a joke could make her feel downcast. Alex, of course, could not realise how much she longed to share his life, even in a little thing like this.

Then came the morning when Beverley awoke with a new sense of exhilaration. For a moment she lay blinking at the ceiling, wondering what could be special about this day. Then she remembered. She jumped out of bed, ran to the window and pulled back the curtains. The tide was in and the sun sparkled and glanced off the wave tips. The sky seemed a vast arch of blue enamel. The herring gulls glided tranquilly in the soft breeze. It was a blue-and-gold day, she decided, and the ball at Kinneil Castle would round it off perfectly.

She dressed quickly, her mind speeding ahead. Today would be no ordinary day. But first she must prepare Alex's breakfast before he went to Solan.

But when she went downstairs she found him there and to her surprise he was actually making an effort to set the table. 'Well, I must say you're becoming quite domesticated!' she told him.

'Why the sound of astonishment in your voice?' he asked. 'For all you know I may have all sorts of hidden talents.'

'Well, setting tables certainly *isn't* one of them,' she told him, as she straightened the cutlery and smoothed out the wrinkles in the tablecloth.

'And may I remind you that, in spite of Morag's instructions, the pease brose is still lumpy.'

'It won't be this morning,' she assured him, as she went into the kitchen.

The kettle hummed on the Aga cooker and it took her no more than a few minutes to blend the pease meal in a little cold water, making sure that the paste was smooth, and then to add the boiling water. She beat it energetically, making sure it was smooth before she cooked it for a short while. When it had thickened and turned a rich dark brown she added a lump of butter and a sprinkling of salt. She served out a generous portion in a heated bowl, picked up a jug of milk and returned to the parlour.

Alex had taken his place, and regarded her offering with approval. 'Just what the doctor ordered!' he remarked appreciatively. 'Not a lump in sight and just the right amount of salt and butter.'

'And a jug of creamy milk,' she reminded him, as she placed it on the table.

In the kitchen once more, she was humming softly to herself as she toasted baps. She kept an eagle eye on them and when they were an even golden brown she turned them over and toasted the other side. They were supplied by a local baker who made them in the traditional Scottish way, and nearly every household in Kinneil had them for breakfast. Spread with butter and honey they were delicious.

Beverley prepared Alex's breakfast before her own and by the time she settled herself at the table sipping from a cup of tea he was already well into a plate of sausage, bacon and egg.

'Did I actually hear you singing in the kitchen?' he asked, 'You're usually rather grumpy in the mornings. But then I suppose there's something special about today.'

'You haven't forgotten that the ball's this evening?' she asked.

'No, not exactly,' he admitted, 'but it doesn't seem to have affected me in the same way.'

'You're used to it,' she told him. 'You go every year. But this is the first time for me. I've never been at an affair of this sort before. And Kinneil Castle is such a wonderful background—a turreted castle hundreds of years old!'

'The ballroom isn't as old as the rest of the building,' he told her. 'It was built in Victorian times, but I must admit they tried to make it look as authentic as possible.'

'I don't mind what period it belongs to,' she told him happily. 'I shouldn't even have known if you hadn't told me.'

He had glanced at her plate. 'It seems to me you're having rather an austere breakfast.'

'Yes, I've lots of things to do today. But later on when I've organised something for you to eat and you're safely off to Solan I'll settle down and have a good tuck-in.'

'And what are all the important things you have to do today?'

'No need to sound so indulgent, as though you were speaking to an over-excited child!' she told him severely. 'But since you ask—well, for one thing I must get my hair done, and I'll probably be kept there for ages. Alison told me she's had to take on two extra girls to cope with the rush of bookings. When I heard that nearly everyone in Kinneil goes to the ball I could hardly believe it, but it seems to be true. So I'm going to give the house a lick and a promise this morning and go down to Alison's as soon as possible.'

'It will give you the chance of a good gossip too,' Alex

remarked. 'Alison has the reputation of always having the lastest news at her fingertips.' He got up from the table reluctantly and stretched lazily. 'I only wish I had an excuse for staying away from work today,' he remarked. 'But since I haven't could you raise my spirits by telling me what's going to be in my lunch-box today?'

Beverley smiled a little smugly. 'I prepared a lamb stew last night, just the way you like it, with lots of vegetables and thick gravy.'

'And what's for afters?'

'Chocolate sandwich with real fresh cream,' she told him.

As she handed him the plastic boxes containing the food she warned him, 'Remember, warm the stew properly. You're not to leave it there all day long and then eat it cold so that all my work is gone for nothing.'

'I'll remember,' he promised, as he bent down and kissed her quickly on the top of her head. 'You know, Beverley,' his voice had softened subtly, 'I'm really looking forward to tonight. There'll be just you and I in a world of our own.'

She gazed up at him, her eyes bright. 'How are we to manage it in that ballroom packed with nearly everybody in Kinneil?'

'As far as I'm concerned it won't matter how many people are there,' he told her, his voice low and tender. 'They'll see you in my arms, but all the time you'll be tucked safely in my heart.'

She stood at the door watching his receding figure as he strode towards the jetty. Before he disappeared from view he turned and waved briefly. So he had known that she would be standing there gazing after him until the last possible minute! And as she finally went indoors she was thinking that it was impossible to appear cool and sophisticated when one was head over heels in love.

She whisked through the rooms in record time, giving

them, as she had told Alex, a lick and a promise. There would be plenty of time to tidy them thoroughly after the ball was over. She prepared the evening meal and popped it into a slow oven, then set off for the village.

Alison's little salon was packed and, as she opened the door, Beverley was greeted by the almost deafening sound of voices raised over the noise of the hair-driers. Alison herself was busily wielding a drier as she gave a blow-wave to a customer, and her two assistants were working furiously. A row of chairs against a wall was nearly filled by waiting customers, but there was a vacant place at the end and Beverley took this, picked up a magazine and resigned herself to a long delay before she could be attended to.

Alison, in spite of being so busy, kept a keen eye on everything that occurred in her little establishment and during a lull in the frantic pace she took the opportunity of whispering to Beverley, 'Hang on! We'll try to get through this lot as quickly as possible. By the way, I've an interesting bit of gossip about her ladyship herself.'

Beverley looked at her enquiringly and she lowered her voice as she turned away, 'Yes, Miss Lynne Redfern herself.'

Beverley was a little surprised when she heard the bitter tone with which Alison spoke, because the two girls had seemed to be on good terms. And as she waited Beverley was wondering what on earth Alison could have to tell her about Lynne. Whatever it was, it could have nothing to do with herself, she was thinking thankfully. There was nothing Lynne could now say or do that could be a threat to her new-found happiness.

When at last it came her turn to be attended to, Beverley found that Alison seemed to have forgotten her promise of news about Lynne. Instead she stood back and regarded Beverley critically. 'Have you any particular style in mind for tonight?' she enquired.

'No, I thought of wearing it pretty much as it is,' Beverley admitted. 'Just getting it shampooed and set, you know.'

Alison pursed her lips. 'Well, what I feel is that wearing it loose about your shoulders is too casual for the do at the Castle. What do you say to soft waves in front and the back swept into a French knot? It would add a touch of sophistication.'

Beverley surveyed herself critically in the mirror trying to visualise how Alison's suggestion would look with her new evening dress. 'Yes, I think I'd like to try it,' she said at last. 'I've worn this style for a while now. Perhaps it's time for something different.'

Alison set to work at once and was soon engrossed in producing exactly the effect she had in mind. Apparently she had forgotten her promise to pass on a titbit of gossip about Lynne, and Beverley wondered how she was going to jog her memory.

'I suppose Lynne Redfern hasn't been here today,' she remarked.

'Not likely,' Alison returned. 'Not when she's sent to Fort William for a hairdresser to come to the Castle to attend to herself and the guests who are staying with her! Oh, by the way,' she added in a brighter tone, 'everyone is talking about it.'

'About what?' Beverley asked.

'It's just a rumour, of course,' Alison went on, 'but they do say Lynne is going to announce her engagement at the ball.'

'Engagement?' Beverley queried.

'Of course it may be only talk,' Alison said quickly. 'You know how these silly rumours fly about at times.'

'Is there any talk about who the man is?' Beverley asked, keeping her voice as calm as possible.

Alison made a great business of rolling a curler into

Beverley's hair, but Beverley had the curious feeling that even before she spoke she knew exactly what Alison was about to say.

'It could be anyone, of course,' Alison replied, 'Lynne always has a crowd of admirers around her, but they do say it's Alex Ramage. After all, he's the man she really cares for.'

CHAPTER FOURTEEN

BEVERLEY stared at her own reflection in the mirror and hoped Alison had not noticed how pale she had become. 'Lynne engaged to Alex Ramage!' she repeated. 'But——'

It was with an effort she prevented herself crying out, But Alex is going to marry me!

Luckily Alison was hurrying on. 'Yes, there's been a lot of talk about who it could be, but it's as plain as the nose on my face that she's crazy about him. And Lynne always gets her own way! It's easy to see why she's fallen for him, for there's something very attractive about him. Although I must say I'm not altogether keen on that arrogant manner of his!' Alison laughed. 'I'd say, though, as far as Lynne is concerned, his manner is part of his fascination.'

Beverley moistened her dry lips. Wild thoughts tumbled through her mind. What could this extraordinary news mean? At one moment it seemed to her to be completely senseless. Next moment Alison's words were ringing through her brain. 'Lynne always gets her own way.' Was it possible that even now, when she was so certain that it was she herself whom Alex loved, Lynne could snatch him away from her? It was such a short time since she had thought that it no longer mattered what Lynne said or did. Now, once again, she had assumed a terrifying importance.

And now there was no interest for Beverley in the transformation Alison was effecting in her appearance. As her dark hair was swept into deep shining waves and curved into a wide loose roll that ran from the top of her head to the nape of her neck, her appearance, formerly softly youthful, was given a touch of almost classical severity.

She stood up, feeling numb and without enthusiasm, but as she saw the expression of eager pleasure on Alison's face she exerted herself to express appreciation. 'Thanks, Alison,' she said as warmly as she could. 'You've done wonders! I'm so pleased you suggested it.'

'Yes, I think it is a success,' Alison said with satisfaction. 'And I'll have an eye out for you this evening to see how it goes with your dress. I'll know then if we've really done the right thing.'

Beverley had hardly left the hairdresser's when she saw Lynne's tall graceful figure advancing along the short village street. She looked around wildly. Was there time to bolt into MacKenzie's store and hide herself there behind the revolving racks of paperbacks or among the counters heaped with their miscellany of goods? At that moment she felt that to have to make polite conversation with Lynne was more than she could bear. Not while her mind was so confused and disorientated by Alison's extraordinary news!

But Lynne had already seen her. Her eyes widened as she caught sight of Beverley's new hair-style. With a few of her long swinging strides she approached. 'What a pretty hair-do! Don't tell me you got it done in Alison's?'

Beverley nodded and forced her lips into a smile. 'Yes, I think it looks rather more sophisticated than my usual style,' she found herself babbling.

'I should say so!' Lynne agreed. 'You know, now that I see it, I regret I didn't have my own done by Alison. But Daddy has arranged for a man to come from Fort William to attend to our guests, and naturally I must let him do mine too.'

There was a short pause after this and Beverley became aware that Lynne was regarding her with interest. 'My, but you do look pale,' she remarked.

'Yes, it was rather hot in Alison's this morning,' Beverley said quickly. Then, to distract Lynne's attention from herself, she asked, 'I suppose Mandy has gone home?'

'Yes, I saw her off myself,' Lynne replied. 'Such a relief to be rid of her at last! The child is a dreadful responsibility. And no matter how nice I try to be to her, she really doesn't like me.' She laughed shortly. 'But you and Alex seem quite to have won her heart. She wanted to come over and say goodbye to you before she went, but I put a stopper on that. It would be just like Mandy to get into mischief on the very day she was to go home!'

Listening to her, Beverley was struck with wonder. What a strange girl Lynne was! How coolly she was chatting of hair-styles and of Mandy's departure, if in fact this was the day on which her engagement was to be announced. But perhaps Alison's gossip was all nonsense and there was no foundation whatsoever for the rumour. Suddenly Beverley felt she simply had to know. But she was still too confused to approach the subject skilfully, and to her horror she heard herself blurt, 'You hear the strangest things at Alison's! The latest is that your engagement is to be announced this evening at the ball.'

She could hear the tremor in her own voice, and hoped Lynne had not noticed.

'Most hairdressers gossip, I suppose,' Lynne replied, 'but Alison seems to take the cake. Well, as it happens, she's right.'

'You mean, you really are—are going to announce your engagement?' Beverley heard herself stutter.

Lynne smiled faintly, her eyes fixed on Beverley's anxious face, 'Yes, and wouldn't you just like to know who's the lucky man?'

Beverley swallowed. 'You mean, you're—you're going to keep it a secret—until tonight?'

'That's exactly what I mean. It will have more impact then. Don't you agree?' And with a wave of her hand Lynne turned away and continued her stroll along the street.

Beverley, as she made her way back to the guesthouse, was thinking how strangely the morning had turned out. Such a short time previously she had been full of happy expectations for the future. Now she felt only a leaden misery. How calm and self-possessed Lynne had been, so sure that whatever she wanted would happen. She was in love with Alex and did not see how anything or anyone could stand in the way of her achieving what she wanted.

Beverley turned in at the gate of the guesthouse and went along the narrow path. But instead of going into the house, she walked across the short fine grass to the swinging hammock-seat. Somehow out here in the fresh air, with the beauty of Isa's wonderful garden around her, it seemed easier to face this crisis in her life.

After a few moments she forced herself to turn her thoughts to something she had been thrusting into the background of her mind. Where did Alex stand in all this? He had shown her so clearly that he loved her—surely it was not possible that he had been deceiving her! It seemed incredible. And suddenly, with a wonderful sense of relief, she realised that it *was* incredible. She knew in her heart without a shadow of a doubt that Alex loved her. Lynne, and Lynne alone, had dreamed up this gambit of a public

announcement of an engagement in an effort to force hi
hand.

Only too clearly could Beverley visualise the situation
The crowded ballroom at the height of the festivities. A
dance coming to an end and Mr and Mrs Redfern takin,
the centre of the floor. 'It gives us great happiness to an
nounce the engagement of our daughter,' Mr Redfer
would begin.

Or was Lynne modern enough to make the announce
ment herself?

How easy it would be for her to manage it, so that
Alex found himself in a situation he had never envisaged. After they had danced together—and after all,
he would have to give his hostess a dance—as the
music came to a stop, she would say, 'Just a moment,
Alex,' detaining him in the centre of the room while
the other dancers retired to the seats around the floor.
Then, 'Ladies and gentlemen, or should I just call you
friends, I have the most wonderful news, Alex and I
have decided to get married and I want you all to be the
first to know.' Her face would be tilted then for Alex's
kiss.

Beverley sprang to her feet. At least Alex should be
warned! She would go to Solan immediately and tell him
what Lynne had in mind.

She ran into the house and up the stairs to her bedroom,
pulled out a pair of canvas shoes and thrust her feet into
them, setting the elegant shoes which she had worn to the
village spinning into the corner of the room. Her next
thought was to check if the sandy causeway to Solan was
clear. She rushed to the window. But the channel between
the two islands was still full. It would be another hour
before she would be able to walk across. She prowled about
her room like a caged thing, burning with impatience at
the delay.

But as she waited she had time to think things over, and

in the end she decided not to go. She could rest secure in
Alex's love. He would know how to deal with the situation
when it arose. She could safely leave everything to him.
Besides—and this was a thought that made her heart
beat faster—if she went to Solan and told him what Lynne
had in mind, how could she ever be sure that she had not
forced his hand? Far better that he should freely choose
between them.

But all the joy she had experienced in anticipating the
ball had quite evaporated and in it's place was strain and
unhappiness.

When Alex returned that evening he was in high spirits.
It was clear that he had put aside the cares of his profession
and that he intended to enjoy the evening to the full. He
laughed and chatted while he ate the meal she had prepared for him and afterwards sat by the fire smoking his
pipe. And Beverley did her best to hide her depression by
replying rather feverishly to his remarks and by gusts of
forced laughter.

No matter how often she told herself that her fears
were groundless, she had a strange dread of Lynne, a curious feeling of helplessness, as though that beautiful
girl with the green eyes had witch-like powers that could
charm Alex away from her, no matter how deeply he loved
her.

Into her mind flashed pictures from the times when she
and Alex had been together on Solan and she found herself
reliving those cherished moments as if this evening would
see them evaporate for ever.

She was vaguely aware that Alex was talking to her, but
her thoughts were so deeply engrossed with the past that
she hardly heard.

'You know, Beverley, you aren't listening to a word I
say.' Alex got to his feet. 'We may as well get into our glad
rags, I suppose, because you're not going to pay any attention to me until we're on our way.'

She dressed with care, taking time over her make-up and arranging her hair exactly as Alison had done. As she slid a grip into the depths of a wave she was wondering what style Lynne would wear. At that moment the hairdresser at the Castle would be going from one guest to another adding the final touches to their coiffures.

When she was ready she wound a thin gold chain around her neck—her only ornament—and stood in front of the long mirror examining her reflection critically. Yes, the severity of her new hair-do complemented the smooth flowing lines of her dress; each might have been especially designed for the other. And she herself had never looked better, she had to admit to herself. There was a heightened colour in her cheeks, and her eyes were wide and sparkling. She took up the short fur jacket that Morag had loaned her for the evening and went downstairs.

Alex was waiting for her and as she saw the expression on his face as he caught sight of her, she knew that, for this evening at any rate, she was beautiful. 'You look as if you'd stepped out of the illustration to a fairy-tale,' he told her.

'You look different too!' she smiled, as she saw the black velvet coat with the silver diamond-shaped buttons, the gleam of the hilt of the *skean dhu*, the shirt of finest material with its lace jabot, the kilt with its vivid jewel-like colours. The romantic Scottish outfit suited his tall sturdy figure to perfection: against it the rugged, uncompromising cast of his face became handsome.

Beverley smiled up at him, linked her arm in his, and it was with a sort of feverish gaiety that she went out with him to the car he had hired for the evening.

As they drove along the bumpy primitive road tall bushes of white and coral-pink hawthorn by the wayside filled the car with exquisite heady perfume. Then came their first glimpse of the Castle, seeming this evening to float against a pale lemon-yellow sky, its windows filled with golden light. As the car turned in through the great wrought-iron gates and progressed along the drive the giant bushes of rhododendron on either side were starred with clusters of great yellow and red and palest greenish-white blossoms.

As Alex stopped the car in the glowing patch of golden light that flowed out to the great gravelled space before the building, they could hear the sound of romantic music played by an orchestra. Beverley knew that entertainers had also been hired and a group of folk singers, so that every taste might be catered to during the evening.

'Happy?' He smiled down at her as they got out of the car.

'Oh, wonderful!' She forced a note of eagerness into her voice. 'I wouldn't have missed this for anything!'

He glanced at her doubtfully for a moment. 'You're in a strange mood this evening, Beverley. I only hope you *are* happy!'

How impossible it was to deceive Alex, she was thinking. And how impossible to let him know the cause of her unhappiness!

But his question showed her that she must exert herself to put up a pretence of enjoying herself.

As they were welcomed by Mr and Mrs Redfern, Beverley was struck by the contrast between Lynne and her parents, both of whom were short and rather stocky in build. Mr Redfern's clothes were well-tailored and expensive, but Mrs Redfern was dressed unbecomingly in a stiff satin gown. But it was obvious that both of them were very happy, and Beverley was touched to see how proudly they glanced at their tall slender daughter who appeared so self-possessed and poised in her dress of coral-red chiffon.

Soon Beverley and Alex were dancing, and she was

surprised to find how light he was on his feet and how ideally their steps matched.

Lynne as she moved about among her guests was surrounded by a group of young admirers, in particular Ian Laird, whose eyes never seemed to leave his young hostess.

As the evening wore on Beverley found herself chatting with many of the people she had met since coming to the Islands. There was Donald MacKenzie, looking so spruce in his kilt. There was Alison, her glorious chestnut-red hair shining, accompanied by her husband, home from the Navy. Alison wore a white dress with a tartan sash across the shoulder and fastened with a jewelled brooch.

'I've been patting myself on the back about your new hairstyle,' she told Beverley. 'Considering I hadn't seen your dress it's amazing how well it goes with it. You'd think I designed it with that wonderful dress in mind.'

'You see, you're the belle of the ball,' Alex told her later as they danced together again. And Beverley could not but agree in her heart that her dress had made a great impression.

Lynne too congratulated her. 'I must say I didn't think Morag was capable of turning out anything so out of the ordinary,' she told Beverley. 'It makes my poor chiffon look quite a rag.'

Shortly afterwards came the moment Beverley had been dreading. While Alex partnered his hostess, Beverley sat out the dance. What a well-matched couple they were, she was thinking—both so tall, and Lynne's slender figure seeming so perfectly to complement Alex's height and broad build.

As the dance came to an end they chanced to be within earshot and Beverley heard Lynne say regretfully. 'That was wonderful, Alex! Oh well, all good things come to an end sooner or later, don't they? Or don't you feel that way about it?'

Whatever Alex replied was lost to Beverley as a little group of people near to her burst into animated chatter. But a moment later Lynne was claimed by Ian Laird for the next dance and Alex came towards her.

So the moment she had so much dreaded had passed away and nothing had happened! Lynne must be going to leave the announcement to her father.

Supper time came and they strolled into the room in which the buffet had been set out. Here the air was scented with exquisite blooms from the hothouses. Great baskets full of luscious fruits were placed at intervals along the buffet tables which were laden with every sort of dish, some of them so intricately garnished that it seemed a pity to cut into them. And Beverley delighted in the baskets of spun sugar ornamented with tiny roses of pink and yellow.

She left Alex to choose for her among the bewildering array of delicious foods and soon found that he had no compunction in indicating to the waiter in attendance that he wanted portions from some of the most exquisitely decorated dishes.

They had their meal at one of the little tables that had been placed in the bays of the windows. Here they could look out over the gardens where the lanterns shone among the shrubs and were hung on the branches of the slender birch trees.

Afterwards they decided to join the many guests who were having a stroll in the gardens. There was a slight chilliness in the air and at Alex's suggestion Beverley went to collect the fur jacket Morag had lent her.

Before one of the mirrors in the big room which had been set aside as a cloakroom for the ladies, Beverley found Lynne. As she saw Beverley pick up the fur jacket she said quickly, 'You're not leaving already, are you? You're not bored?'

'No, of course not!' Beverley replied. 'We're just going to have a stroll in the grounds.' She paused a little awkwardly. 'I'd like to see the lanterns. I—well, I'm wondering if I hung them in the best spots.'

Lynne's smiled was a little crooked as she said, 'Dear me, yes. I'm sure you're interested in the lanterns. Well, don't be too long, because there's the announcement of my engagement, you know.'

'Oh yes!' To cover her agitation, Beverley seated herself before one of the mirrors, took out a comb and tried to appear engrossed in arranging her hair.

But Lynne was not deceived. 'And to put you out of your misery,' she said in a loud harsh voice, 'I may as well tell you that it's Ian Laird I'm marrying.'

'Oh!' The comb fell from Beverley's fingers and she was glad of the opportunity to bend down and pick it up.

'So I was right this morning,' Lynne swung around to face her, 'when I thought you were worried in case it was Alex! Well, there was only one small difficulty there, and that was that he's never asked me to marry him. And the evening you and he came from Solan—I'm speaking about the day Mandy was lost—I knew that he never would. I could see it was you he was in love with, and little Lynne is not one to wait around and beg and plead with a man who's in love with another girl. I must say I think everything would have been different if you'd never come here,' she added. 'I think tonight my engagement would have been announced to Alex. But you did come. And I'm not a girl to cry over what might have been. What I need is a man who's very much in love with me. Ian is, so I'm marrying him.'

'I—I wish you every happiness,' Beverley told her in a small voice. The relief was so great that she felt as if she could hardly breathe.

But Lynne's green eyes had missed nothing. 'So you actually thought I'd try to tie Alex's hands by announcing

that I was engaged to him! You may be in love with him—
and I don't doubt that you are,' she went on contemptuously, 'but you've a lot to learn about him if you think for
one moment Alex would stand for such a thing.'

When Beverley could find no reply to this, Lynne stood
up. 'Coming?' she asked.

Together they went downstairs, Lynne with her head
thrown back, proud and defiant.

As Beverley rejoined Alex she found the ballroom buzzing with the news that Lynne's engagement was to be
announced shortly. The guests were gathering with cham-
pagne glasses in their hands, and shortly afterwards Mr
Redfern made the announcement. Beverley watched
Alex's face as he joined in the toast and could see no sign of
regret in it.

It was with contentment in her heart that she went out
with him into the grounds.

Such a wonderful night! she was thinking. The moon
had risen and cast a silvery glow over everything. Everywhere there was the scent of flowers. They strolled forward
until they came to a high spot under a cluster of trees from
which they could look out over the sea and see Solan
floating on the still moonlit waters, like an enchanted
island.

'Tell me, Beverley,' he asked softly, 'do you regret
that tomorrow all this will be over and we shall be back
to work on that island that looks so beautiful from
here?'

'No,' she said slowly. 'Tonight is wonderful, of course.
But I like our black house out there on Solan. After all, it
must have been a Kinneil Castle to some family at one
time. People lived out their lives there, had their joys and
sorrows there. Anyway, I'm not one of those people who
feel a party should go on for ever. I'd grow tired of it after a
while.'

'I'm glad to hear you say that,' he told her, 'because

there's something I want to ask you. Do you think that any girl could be happy married to a man who lives the sort of life I do? And remember it wouldn't always be Solan. There would be trips abroad to study wild-life in far distant countries. To mosquito-ridden rivers in New Guinea, or the burning deserts of central Australia. She would have to be a very special sort of girl, one who wouldn't be afraid to face what lay ahead. And above all a girl who would be prepared to put up with me!'

He waited, and when Beverley had found her voice, she replied, 'Yes, I believe you could find that sort of girl, Alex. But——'

'Yes?' he asked.

'But I'm afraid she would have her faults too! Might be a bit—well, a bit quick-tempered, perhaps.'

'A girl who would throw a tea-cup at a man, perhaps, and tell him exactly what she thought of him?'

'Something like that!' she admitted.

'Look, Beverley, you and I have been a couple of fools, quarrelling and wasting our precious time when we should have been loving one another. But that's a mistake we won't make again. You see, we've already got over the quarrels most couples have after they're married. Our times at the black house have taught us a lot about each other. We know what we're in for.'

'Do we?' she asked. 'Really, Alex, don't you think you're taking too much for granted?'

'Come, Beverley, we're not going to have a fight now, are we?' he asked, and she noted with satisfaction that he sounded quite alarmed.

'You're talking as if I were the girl you want, but you haven't asked me to marry you,' she told him crisply.

'Why, you little donkey, of course I'm asking you to marry me!'

He sounded quite exasperated and Beverley found it hard to restrain a laugh.

Alex tilted her chin towards him. 'You little devil, I believe you're deliberately picking a quarrel with me—even now!'

But whatever she would have had to say to this was silenced by his kiss.

Harlequin Plus

THE ISLE OF SKYE

Skye is the largest of the Inner Hebrides, a group of islands lying just off the northwest coast of Scotland. Fishing, the distilling of whiskey, and cattle and sheep raising constitute the mainstays of life on this irregularly shaped, scenic island—though in recent years tourism here has grown by leaps and bounds.

Serious climbers challenge the Cuillins, Skye's misty jagged mountains, while other visitors enjoy pony trekking, sailing, hiking, cycling and exploring. And there's much to explore: ancient standing stones, Norse hilltop forts, the haunting ruins of old clan strongholds, and the harbor of Portree, Skye's capital, noted for its manufacture of beautiful tweeds, tartans and woolens.

Another must-see is Dunvegan castle, ancestral home of Clan Macleod and Scotland's oldest inhabited castle—it has been occupied since being built in the ninth century!

Skye's most romantic historical figure is probably Flora Macdonald. Gentleman's daughter and plucky heroine of the eighteenth century, she disguised a prince as her serving maid and helped him escape the English soldiers pursuing him. The prince was Charles Edward Stuart, "Bonnie Prince Charlie," and that incident was immortalized in the lovely Skye Boat Song:

> Speed, bonnie boat, like a bird on the wing
> "Onward," the sailors cry
> Carry the lad that's born to be king
> Over the sea to Skye.

Harlequin Presents...

**Stories to dream about...
Stories of love...**

...all-consuming, passionate love,
the way you've always imagined it,
the way you know it should be!

SUPERROMANCE

Longer, exciting, sensual and dramatic!

Fascinating love stories that will hold
you in their magical spell till the last page
is turned!

Now's your chance to discover the earlier
books in this exciting series. Choose from
the great selection on the following page!

Choose from this list of great
SUPERROMANCES!

SUPERROMANCE

Complete and mail this coupon today!

- -

Harlequin Reader Service

In the U.S.A.
1440 South Priest Drive
Tempe, AZ 85281

In Canada
649 Ontario Street
Stratford, Ontario N5A 6W2

Please send me the following SUPERROMANCES. I am enclosing my check or money order for $2.50 for each copy ordered, plus 75¢ to cover postage and handling.

- ☐ #1 END OF INNOCENCE
- ☐ #2 LOVE'S EMERALD FLAME
- ☐ #3 THE MUSIC OF PASSION
- ☐ #4 LOVE BEYOND DESIRE
- ☐ #5 CLOUD OVER PARADISE
- ☐ #6 SWEET SEDUCTION
- ☐ #7 THE HEART REMEMBERS
- ☐ #8 BELOVED INTRUDER

Number of copies checked @ $2.50 each =	$_____
N.Y. and Ariz. residents add appropriate sales tax	$_____
Postage and handling	$_____.75
TOTAL	$_____

I enclose_____ .
(Please send check or money order. We cannot be responsible for cash sent through the mail.)
Prices subject to change without notice.

NAME_____
(Please Print)

ADDRESS_____

CITY_____

STATE/PROV._____

ZIP/POSTAL CODE_____

Offer expires May 31, 1982   109563323